BKM
3/97   WESTERN
BMc

DW

NEWARK PUBLIC LIBRARY-NEWARK, OHIO 43055
3 2487 00400 6475

Y0-CZS-769

WITHDRAWN

```
Large Print Sho
Short, Luke, 1908-1975.
A man could get killed
```

3558

7-14

AUG 0 1 1996

STACKS

NEWARK PUBLIC LIBRARY
NEWARK, OHIO

3558

GAYLORD M

A MAN COULD GET KILLED

Also Published in Large Print
from G.K. Hall by Luke Short:

High Vermilion
Station West
Bought With A Gun
Stalkers
Savage Range

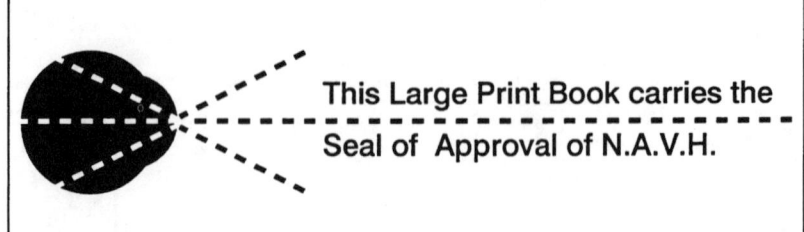

A MAN COULD GET KILLED

LUKE SHORT

G.K. Hall & Co.
Thorndike, Maine

Copyright © 1980 by Luke Short

All rights reserved.

Published in 1995 by arrangement with Kate Hirson and Daniel Glidden.

G.K. Hall Large Print Western Collection.

The text of this Large Print edition is unabridged.
Other aspects of the book may vary from the original edition.

Set in 16 pt. News Serif by Minnie B. Raven.

Printed in the United States on permanent paper.

Library of Congress Cataloging in Publication Data

Short, Luke, 1908–1975.
    A man could get killed / Luke Short.
      p.   cm.
    ISBN 0-7838-1461-5 (lg. print : hc)
    1. Large type books.   I. Title.
PS3513.L68158M33   1995
813'.54—dc20   95-24420

A MAN COULD GET KILLED

One

Regular passengers on the lone coach of the Primrose & Northern mixed train knew that the water stop at the Long Reach tank was always a short one, so they did not bother, this night, to get out and stretch their legs.

To make sure that no one else did, the brakeman came through the half-filled coach where a third of the passengers were asleep, intoning quietly, "Just a water stop, folks."

The two men seated beside each other both looked at the brakeman, and then, when he was past them, the small dark man closest to the window said, "He's new."

The other man, older and also dressed in clean range clothes, said dryly, "He's the only thing new on this wreck of a railroad."

This was the last conversation they were destined to have with each other.

Outside the car, now quiet, they could hear the sound of a horse walking slowly down the length of the car in the chill September night. Morton Schaeffer, the man next to the window, turned his head to look out and, of course could see nothing because of the reflection on the window of the coach's overhead lamps. Deputy Marshal Newford did not look out, but lazily eyed the retreating figure of the brakeman. Then the horse stopped walking.

A second later, the roar of a shotgun erupted out in the night. Simultaneously came the sound of shattering glass. Mort Schaeffer caught the shot full in the face. He was dead before the sound reached his brain. The force of the shot drove him into Marshal Newford, who, with a strangled cry, raised his left hand to his left eye.

A lone man, in the seat ahead of the pair, jumped to his feet, turned, saw Schaeffer's mangled face, and fainted. By the time the brakeman had run back down the aisle, Morton had rolled to the floor and Newford was trying to staunch the flow of blood from his left eye. It was only then that the passengers, some talking, some shouting started to become aware of what had happened.

The same train and the same coach, three weeks later, brought Deputy U.S. Marshal Sam Kennery into the big brick station at Junction City, this new state's capital. Kennery was not aware that his seat on the night train from the north was only one removed from the seat where Schaeffer had been ambushed. Kennery was a stranger to this country, and he did not even know that Morton Schaeffer had been killed.

As the train ground to a halt abreast of the station platform, four women, talked-out after a long journey, came down the aisle, eager to be greeted on the dark platform by their menfolk and children. Sam Kennery remained seated until they were past, then rose, yawned, and stretched his more than six feet of hard-muscled frame. Afterwards, he reached down, removed the rumpled newspaper that had been covering his dust-colored Stetson, and restored the hat's proper center crease with big, long-fingered hands. He was a man of thirty, dressed in a duck jacket over a calico shirt, and the commoner's boots he wore held a dull polish — which, in itself, was a mild deception since they were seldom polished. His face, however, held no deception; it was lean, weather-burned a few shades darker than his pale, thick, shortcut hair. His very blue eyes held a veiled alertness above a thin nose that a ham-handed army surgeon had reset imperfectly after it was broken. Its ridge had a slight jog near the bridge, and Kennery, who looked in a mirror only to shave, had seen it often enough to forget it. His mouth was wide above a deeply cleft chin that had a suggestion of stubbornness about it. He reached up now and pulled down the lashed blanket roll from the overhead rack, lifted his saddle from the floor, and then moved down the now-deserted car to step onto a badly lit platform. A hack, whose legend *Prairie Hotel*, painted on its side, was lit by the carriage lamps, was drawn up to the edge of the platform. When Kennery headed for it, the driver moved toward him to take his blanket roll and saddle. As Kennery handed them to the driver, he said, "Leave them behind the desk. I'll walk."

"We'll have them in your room for you, sir."

Kennery waited until the hack had pulled out before he stepped off the platform and headed toward the town.

The newly finished State House, some fifteen blocks away and perched high on a river bluff, was impossible to mistake in the light of this night's half-moon, and now Sam headed for it. Rather than traveling the main street, he cut off to the west and picked up the residential section, and in turn was picked up by a dog who, after barking, passed him on to a dog in the next block.

He was remembering now the letter from Marshal Wilbarth: "Come to the State House when you get in, and on your way, keep out of sight." It had been a strange letter, a communication — or rather a lack of communication — that baffled and irritated him.

His own boss, Marshal Tom Freed, had been almost as uncommunicative. "We're loaning you to Wilbarth. He'll be in touch with you," Freed had said.

When Kennery had protested that Junction City was not in their judicial district, Freed had asked him, "What do you care? Wilbarth wants a new face, one that isn't known." Further than that, Freed refused to discuss why Wilbarth wanted him. He would say only that the commissioner approved the loan of a deputy to Wilbarth.

The capitol building, as Kennery saw it from the curving brick drive that ran through the capitol grounds, was a massive and imposing three-story stone affair, topped by a gilded dome. Lamps were burning in a few of the second-story offices, and only upon seeing them did Kennery remember that the legislature was in session, with its night committee meetings. Only four years ago, Junction City had been made the state capital, and the first act of its legislature had been to appropriate money for the new capitol building. It was, Sam thought as he mounted the steps, a place that would impress the millionaire mine owner as much as it would the lowliest line rider of this newest state.

Once inside the building, Sam tramped down the marble-floored corridor in search of the basement stairs, according to Freed's instruction. So far, he reflected, he had been seen only by the hack driver and five overprotective dogs.

Descending the stairs, he walked the lower corridor to the room under the governor's office that had a closed door bearing the legend *U.S. Marshal*. He could see a pencil-line of light beneath the door. He knocked and was bade enter.

Kennery stepped into a long, narrow room and halted abruptly at the sight of two men seated across from each other at a long table that held a tall lamp. They were both in shirtsleeves, and the white drift of paper between them told Kennery he had interrupted a conference. Even their expressions told him that. The younger of the two men had a faintly truculent expression on his narrow face, and Sam noted that he wore a black patch over his left eye, held in place by a ribbon that circled his head of dark hair. This would not be Wilbarth, or Freed would have mentioned that he was blind in one eye. His attention shifted to the bigger and older man, and he said quietly, "Evening, Marshal. You wrote me. Name's Kennery."

Marshal Wilbarth rose and, in the act, pushed his chair back. When he was erect, Sam saw that he was a huge man, wide and tall. His hair was as white as his full mustaches, and capped a face that could have been carved out of the same marble that floored the corridors. It was a pale face, stern as any deacon's, and would not, Sam guessed, smile easily. His eyes were gray and chill, but when he moved toward Sam and extended a huge hand, his voice was friendly, almost gentle. "Glad you're here, Kennery. The train must have been late."

"It was on time. I walked from the depot." They shook hands now, and with his free hand, the marshal gestured toward his companion, saying, "Meet Anse Newford. He's one of my deputies." Newford rose, and he and Sam shook hands briefly across the table.

"Notice anyone hanging around the depot?" the marshal asked.

"Didn't look. Was I supposed to?"

Wilbarth sighed and said, "I don't reckon. Sit down. Take off your coat if you want."

"If you mean was I followed, I wasn't," Sam said.

"That's what I wanted to know," Wilbarth said dryly.

Keeping his coat on, Sam sat down in the barrel chair, half-facing Wilbarth, who was still standing. Then the marshal said with quiet bluntness, "I expected an older man."

Sam said, just as quietly and bluntly, "That's one department where I can't accommodate you, Marshal."

Wilbarth accepted this unsmilingly, but the hint of a grin touched Newford's shadowed face.

Now Wilbarth seated himself. "Did Freed tell you why you're loaned to us?"

Sam shook his head in negation. "Your letter didn't tell me anything, so Freed didn't. He probably figured that was the way you wanted it."

Wilbarth seemed not to have heard, for his expression of resigned disappointment did not change. He only said to Newford, "Tell him, Anse."

In a dry, unemotional tone of voice, Newford told of bringing in a witness by train, and of the ambush at the water tank, in which Schaeffer had lost his life and he himself had lost his eye.

"Witness to what?" Kennery asked, when Newford had finished.

A glint of appreciation came and went in Newford's good eye, and then his glance shifted to the marshal as if he were deferring to the older man.

Wilbarth cleared his throat. "For the past six years, a Texas drover by the name of Big Dad Herrington has had the beef contract for the Indians on the reservation up north. The Indian agent's name up there is Con Brayton. Between the two of them, they've milked the government out of tens of thousands of dollars. Herrington would drive up there and deliver, say, fifteen hundred head. Brayton would pay him for three thousand. Herrington would return him half the difference. In six years that came to a pretty sizeable chunk of money.

"Schaeffer knew this, that's why he was killed?" Sam asked.

Wilbarth nodded. "Schaeffer always received the herds and kept the tally. He was an agency employee. A white man married to an Indian."

"Was Schaeffer in on it?" Sam asked.

Wilbarth pointed a finger at Newford, and at this signal, his deputy took up the story. "No he wasn't, but he got suspicious toward the end. Brayton would order the herd split up into a dozen small herds, to be scattered all over the reservation. He'd appoint Indian herders, and even if they could count, they wouldn't bother to. Brayton claimed that the grass for miles around the agency was grazed out. What he really wanted was to scatter the herds so no accurate count could be made, and Schaeffer suspicioned this. He still wouldn't have talked if it hadn't been for one thing: Brayton had a taste for Indian women, and he made a mistake of trying for Schaeffer's wife."

Wilbarth interrupted now. "That's when Schaeffer wrote us. I sent Anse up there and he pieced together what he just told you. Herrington and Brayton were indicted for criminal fraud. Their trial was scheduled for two and a half weeks ago. Schaeffer, of course, was the star witness, and Anse was bringing him down for the trial. Everything looked fine until they stopped to take on water at the Long Reach tank. Since then we've had no case against them. The judge granted us a delay, but Brayton's and Herrington's lawyers are howling for the indictment to be quashed, and the judge can't hold out forever."

Sam shifted in his chair. "Where are Brayton and Herrington now?"

Anse Newford said sourly, "Out on bond. The judge ordered them not to leave the district."

"They're here, then?"

"Oh no," Newford said bitterly. "They're down in Primrose. That's about as far away from this office as they could get and still stay in the district."

Sam frowned in puzzlement. "You want me to go up to the reservation and get more evidence for you?"

"I do not," Wilbarth said flatly, almost angrily. "Why hunt up evidence of fraud when you can turn up evidence of murder? I want that pair hanged."

Sam only nodded, and Anse Newford said softly, "That's a large order, Mr. Sam Kennery. Both Brayton and Herrington have solid gold alibis. They were in a Primrose bar about nine hours by train from where Schaeffer was killed."

Sam grimaced in sympathy, and now looked at Wilbarth. "What's my move, Marshal?"

"I wish I knew, but I don't," Wilbarth said wearily. He leaned forward and continued, "All I can tell you is that both men know all my regular deputies and special deputies. Brayton's and Herrington's attorneys are in the judge's chambers every other day, complaining that their clients are being persecuted by my office. The judge warns me so often that I'm helpless. You're not."

Anse spoke up: "One thing might help you, Kennery. Brayton and Herrington are prime boozers and wenchers."

Sam had already gathered that, and now he asked, "I'm to use my own name?"

The marshal nodded. "They won't have heard of you."

"Who am I? What do I do?"

The marshal looked at Newford, who only shrugged, and Wilbarth's chill glance shuttled back to Sam. "This is the best we could come up with, Kennery. You won't talk about yourself, so that means you've got something in your past that's bad. You're in Primrose waiting for a friend to join you. If you can do it safely, hint that this friend is serving time in the pen — say for a bullion robbery."

"Why did I pick Primrose as the place to meet him?"

"They'll figure that out for themselves. Consolidated, at Primrose, is the biggest mine in the state. There are three or four others in the Raft River Range behind Primrose. That means gold and payrolls. Make out that you've come to where the money is."

Newford snapped his fingers then, as if remembering something. He rose, moved over to one of the two rolltop desks at the rear of the room, opened the drawer to get something from it, and returned to the table. Still standing, he dropped a buckskin pouch on the table in front of Kennery. By the sound of the muted clink of coins, Sam knew this was money for expenses.

Wilbarth said, "When you run out of that, get in touch with us."

"How?"

"Write me," Wilbarth said. "Never show up here unless you've arranged a night appointment with me."

Kennery nodded. "What else should I know?"

"Just one more thing," the marshal said. "Sheriff Morehead in Primrose knows you're coming. He'll get in touch with you. Trust him, he's a good man." Now Wilbarth rose. "The Primrose train leaves at six-thirty every morning. Be on it tomorrow." He extended his hand, and Kennery arose and accepted it.

"I don't have to tell you that we won't be there to see you off," Wilbarth said.

Across the table, Newford rose and watched Sam

pocket the buckskin sack. Newford said, "When things look rough, just remember there's a new grave in the cemetery north of town. It holds a man with no face."

"I'll remember a man with one eye too."

Newford gave him a faint, twisted smile. "Yes, there's that too," he said softly.

Outside in the night, Kennery passed the last of the newly planted trees on the capitol grounds, and took the dirt street that slanted down toward the center of town. No wonder Freed had waited to let Wilbarth explain his reason for requesting a special deputy, Kennery thought wryly. It was the kind of situation that anyone connected with a marshal's office hated. No evidence and ironclad alibis and a wicked pressure of time. Once the judge was forced to set a trial date, and Brayton and Herrington were freed for lack of evidence, the two men would disappear, he was sure. How much time did that leave him? That too was an unknown, he thought.

He moved into the business district, passing dark stores and lighted, noisy saloons, until he came to the Prairie House, a big brick hotel that was the town's best. He resisted the impulse to stop off at the saloon next to the entry lobby. If the watchers that Wilbarth had mentioned were not wild imaginings, the first place they would watch would be the hotels' saloons.

He registered under the incurious gaze of the night clerk, took his key, climbed to his room, found his bag and saddle already there, and went to bed.

Two

It was a sunny morning with a hint of October bite in the air when Kennery stepped out onto the platform of Primrose's frame depot. He moved out of the lazy traffic of passengers, and slacked his blanket roll and saddle onto the platform. Looking around him, he saw that the town was built at the very base of the foothills of the towering Raft River Range. Against the foothills and within easy sight were the hoist frames and mill stacks of the mines and mills that had made Primrose one of the richest mining areas in the state. Kennery spotted the hotel hack at the far end of the platform, and lifting his saddle and blanket roll, he headed for it. To the hack driver of the Primrose House, who took his gear and stored it, he seemed to be just another cattleman dressed in range clothes and half-boots, with a frayed duck jacket over his cotton shirt. A worn holster sagged below the bottom of the jacket, a pair of old leather gloves was stuffed in the jacket's right-hand pocket.

As he had done last night in Junction City, Kennery instructed the driver to take his gear into the lobby because he wanted to walk.

The train pulled ahead toward the mill yards, and now, because he had been seated on the mountain side of the car, Kennery got his first close look at the Raft River, which they had roughly paralleled on the way up from the capital. Kennery could see that the rushing river bisected the town, and this side of the river seemed to belong to the mines and miners. A big, dingy saloon whose sign read *Miner's Rest* was the largest building in a block of shabby saloons, cafes, and dance halls. Walking down toward the bridge that spanned the boiling Raft River, Kennery passed many of the miners, in the rough clothes, bit boots, and round-crowned wool hats that seemed to be their working uniform. Big, high-wheeled ore wagons, empty and full, made up most of the street's traffic.

Crossing the wooden bridge that put him on the south bank of the river, Kennery knew immediately that he was in a different kind of town. Grant Street, the main thoroughfare, was wide and lined with tie rails. Many of these buildings were of brick or stone, and had wooden canopies extending over the plank walk in front of them. Buggies, wagons, and saddle horses clustered at the tie rails while the lazy midmorning wagon and horse traffic ebbed and flowed along the street. It was, Kennery thought, a substantial-seeming cow town. Tall cottonwoods shaded the residential part of town, and as he moved up the street, Kennery saw that the two-story, white-painted Primrose House, with its wide veranda running the length of the building, was the most impressive structure on the street. As he approached the steps, he saw that a couple dozen barrel chairs, some occupied by idlers, were scattered the length of the veranda. Up the street he could see the livery stable, with its wide, arched doorway. This part of the town was his kind of place, he thought, as he mounted the steps and entered the lobby.

The big, carpeted lobby held a scattering of horsehair-and-leather-covered sofas and easy chairs. As Kennery crossed to the desk, he glanced through the closed glass-paned doors into the dining room, and saw waitresses preparing the tables for the noon meal. A gray-faced, middle-aged man stood behind the counter, his back to the key rack, and bade Kennery a civil good morning. Sam returned his greeting and then said, "You have weekly rates here?"

"Certainly," the clerk replied. "Going to stay with us awhile?"

Sam wished he could really answer that question, but he only said, "A week, anyway."

As he was registering, he heard men's laughter behind him, and when he had signed his name, he turned to find its source. At the far end of the lobby, on the upstreet side, was a double door that, standing open, showed a portion of the long mahogany bar and its glistening back mirror.

The clerk spoke to his back, then: "This saddle and blanket roll would be yours, wouldn't they, Mr. Kennery?"

Sam turned and nodded. The clerk had walked out from behind the desk, and now picked up the blanket roll with one hand and the saddle with the other, holding it by its horn. He was headed for the stairs beside the dining room door, and Sam spoke swiftly: "I can find my room if you'll give me my key."

The clerk halted, put down the saddle and blanket roll, reached in his pocket, and extended the key. Sam took it, lifted his saddle and slung it over his shoulder, then stooped down for the blanket roll.

"Thank you," the clerk said quietly. Sam nodded. The clerk understood that Sam was deferring to his age, and was grateful. As Sam climbed the stairs, he wondered if he would get another look at the register, for Herrington's and Brayton's names had not been on the page he signed. It would be foolish to try for that second look and arouse curiosity, he thought, for hadn't Wilbarth said both men were staying at the Primrose House?

In his spare, clean corner room, he washed up and then returned to the lobby, crossed it, and moved into the bar. He saw immediately that affectionate attention had gone into the planning of this room. The bar itself was long and solid, and the brass of its rails and spittoons was shined. On either side of the lobby entrance were round, baize-covered tables, a pair to a side, and the chairs pulled up to them were the same type of barrel chairs as those on the veranda, these polished by the pants seats of a thousand gamblers. The walls were paneled with dark wood and held many photographs, some of horses, some of mines and mills. Sam could see in the bar mirror that four men were seated at the table near the rear. Three other cowmen were bellied up to the bar down the room, and they interrupted their conversation long enough to regard him with a friendly curiosity. The bartender moved away from them and came up to ask Sam's pleasure. He was a red-faced, red-haired man past middle age, and when he had spoken, Sam guessed that he was English or Irish.

Sam ordered his drink, and while the bartender was

pouring it, Sam said, "Nice place you have here."

"Thank you. It's the closest thing to a club we've got."

Sam pointed to the bar mirror and remarked, "With that chunk of glass, you can't have many fights in here."

"They are not allowed here, sir. We move them out into the street." He turned then, and went back down the bar.

Sam drank his whiskey, and was surprised at its golden smoothness. A boom of laughter came from one of the cardplayers. Sam looked at his glass and covertly studied the four men in the mirror. The man with his back to the wall had a face that, to Sam, was a type. It was a thin, still, bleach-eyed face, the face of a touchy, mean Texan in his middle thirties. He was the type that raised the hell in every northern trail town. Certainly the laugh hadn't come from him.

It was the man seated facing the bar who now interested Sam. He was the only hatless man in the room, with pale hair so closely clipped that he looked bald. By contrast, his bushy eyebrows were almost the size of small mustaches, and they seemed to hood his eyes. From what Sam could see of him from the waist up, he was a big man, with wide shoulders and meaty arms under a checked shirt, over which he wore an open vest. The face, too, was a puzzle. It was heavy, but the nose was small and aquiline, the shape of a parrot's beak, with a knifelike ridge. The mouth was wide and loose-lipped, now pursed in concentration. Even as Sam watched, the man played a card, and again there came a bellow of laughter. It was beginning to get on Sam's nerves. Big Dad Herrington? Sam wondered.

Now men began coming in from the street entrance, for their before-dinner drink. The card game broke up, and now Sam caught a brief glimpse of the big man as he moved toward the bar with the others. He had a vast belly topping short, stubby legs, yet the length of his mammoth torso gave him a height well over six feet. The cardplayers had a quick shot of whiskey, then moved past Sam and disappeared through the lobby door. In the bar mirror, Sam saw them cut across the lobby toward the dining room.

Could the first man, the Texan, be Con Brayton? Sam wondered. If so, he and Herrington made a formidable-looking pair. He had his second drink, paid for it, and then moved out into the lobby, his appetite whetted by the liquor.

The dining room doors were open now, and a pretty, Junoesque girl, with blond hair banded on top of her head, was in frowning conversation with a younger girl in the white uniform of a waitress. As Sam moved toward the doors, heading for the hatrack beside them, he heard the younger girl say vehemently, "I don't care, Louise! I won't serve that disgusting beast anymore."

"All right, Tenney," Louise sighed. "Trade with Mary." As Sam approached, Louise looked up at him and smiled. "How are you, Mr. Kennery? Are you alone?"

At Sam's nod, Louise said, "Just follow her."

Sam did so, eyeing the trim figure ahead of him. As she drew out a chair and turned to face him, Sam saw the single ring on her ring finger. Dregs of anger were still in her eyes. She gave him a practiced smile, which wrinkled her small nose in an engaging way, and it brought a smile from him. He sat down, and while she poured a glass of water for him, he studied the menu chalked in large letters on the blackboard by the kitchen door.

"The liver is very good today."

Sam glanced up at her. "Liver is never good. Why do you say that?"

"Because my mother cooked it," the girl said tartly, flushing a little.

"That's family loyalty for you," Sam observed.

Tenney looked at him carefully, sizing him up with eyes of so dark a violet that they seemed black. A fleeting smile started to form on her lips, and she suppressed it.

"I'll make a deal with you," she said. "I'll bring the liver. If you don't like it, don't eat it, and I'll bring you the stew."

Sam hesitated, pretending to ponder this. "What if I eat it all and don't like it? Will you still bring me the stew?"

"More than you can eat." She turned and headed for the kitchen. 'Tenney,' Louise had called her. Strange name, and one Sam had never heard before, but oddly attractive. He looked about the room now, and saw that a scattering of diners — all men — had moved into the room while he was talking with Tenney. His attention, however, rested again on the four men who had first come in. He could hear the big man's periodic laugh over the murmur of conversation in the room, and he decided that it rang as false as an old maid's giggle. An easy laugh was always suspect in his book.

Tenney returned almost immediately with his liver and rings of onion, with a side dish of sweet potatoes half-drowned in brown sugar syrup. Sam was appalled at the combination, and he looked from the plate to Tenney. "Don't watch me. Go get me some coffee, please."

When she left, Sam picked up knife and fork and slashed at the liver, expecting the usual bootsole texture. Instead, it cut like butter and he took the first bite. It was something new for him. It had been cooked in some hot herb that had diminished the liver flavor, blending with it and dominating it.

When Tenney returned with his coffee, she approached his table with a faint smile on her small face. Halting beside the table, she put down the coffee and said, "Do I take it back,"

"Try it and I'll hit you," Sam said. "Is there more?"

She gave a low, throaty chuckle. "All you can eat."

Sam pushed his now-empty plate toward her and said, "Your name's Tenney and there's a disgusting beast in this room, isn't there?"

Surprise washed over the girl's face and she said, "Yes to both your questions, but how did you know?"

"I overheard you talking with Louise. Can you point out the beast to me?"

"Why should I?" Tenney asked cautiously.

"Because the daughter of anyone who can cook like this deserves protection."

Tenney laughed shortly. "And needs it."

Sam said nothing, waiting for her to decide whether or not she would tell him. Finally, as she reached for his plate, she said, "Don't look, but you see those four men over at the wall table behind me?"

"I've already looked."

"The fat one."

"I call him Laughing Johnny," Sam said dryly. "Who is he?"

Tenney said grimly, "Big Dad Herrington from big, big Texas."

"What's he doing here?" Sam asked casually, hiding the satisfaction of his right guess.

"Out on bail for cheating the government out of a lot of money."

"Why is he a beast, Tenney? Oh, my name is Sam Kennery. Yours is Tenney. All right, Tenney, why is he a beast?"

Tenney shook her head as it tried to dismiss a memory, then she said with quiet anger, "My mother and I live in this building. I have to lock my room when she isn't with me. Does that give you some idea?"

"Who owns this place, and why isn't Big Dad thrown out?"

"Louise's father owns it. Mr. Selby. And he doesn't know. You won't tell him, will you?" she asked quickly.

"What's against it?" Sam challenged. "No girl should have to put up with that."

"Promise you won't tell him? He's got a heart that's barely ticking. He'd try to kill Herrington, and Herrington would only kill him. He —" Her head swiveled and now Sam glanced from her to see Louise

Selby halting beside the table.

"Everything all right, Tenney?" she asked.

It was Sam who answered her. "I'm new here, miss. I was just asking my way around."

"I'll tell you anything you'd like to know, Mr. Kennery, but Tenney has customers to wait on."

Tenney fled before Sam could tell her that he really didn't want the second helping. Louise Selby looked at him now, and then smiled. "She is pretty, isn't she?"

"I didn't notice," Sam said with a straight face.

Louise Selby chuckled. "Of course not," she said "Nobody ever does." And she left.

Sam finished his pie, and while he was drinking the last of his coffee, Herrington and his companions rose and moved toward the door, stopping at the high desk beside the door to pay Louise Selby for their meal. Sam finished his coffee and followed them to the desk. Halting in front of it, he put down a coin. "That was a good meal, Miss Louise," he volunteered.

"Thank you. I'll tell the cook."

"You know those men that just went out the door?"

"Two of them," Louise said. "They're staying with us."

"That thin fellow with the light eyes that always looks mad — I think I've seen him somewhere."

"That would be Seeley Carnes. He's the trail boss for the big man, Mr. Herrington."

Sam shook his head. "Doesn't ring a bell, but thanks."

Out in the lobby, Sam got his hat and started for the

stairs. He heard a woman's voice call softly, "Sam Kennery."

He turned to see Tenney, with a small tray in her hand, coming toward him. She halted before him and said. "You won't say anything to Mr. Selby?"

"Nothing but hello," Sam reassured her.

She smiled her thanks and headed for the bar, to fill a drink order for one of the diners inside.

Sam started for the stairs, now feeling some puzzlement over what Louise Selby had told him. Where was Con Brayton? he wondered. Seeley Carnes had undoubtedly been called as a witness for the defense at the trial, and that explained his presence. For the present he had Herrington to work on, and that meant Seeley too, although he had no notion as to how he could meet them. It could be simple enough to invite himself into a poker game with them, when the game was open. Still, that would only be the beginning, for a poker acquaintanceship was one of the most fleeting of associations, and anything but friendly in an open game. He would simply have to watch for any opening to meet them.

In his room, he moved over to the corner where his saddle was stowed away, lifted it and slung it over his shoulder, then headed back downstairs. He had no notion whether he would need a horse or not, but simple caution told him a mount should be available.

At the livery stable, he spent a pleasant hour looking over the horses that were for hire and trying them, and finally he chose a big bay gelding that looked like a stayer. Before he paid for the week's hire of the bay, he made sure that it was to be his horse, available to him at any and all times. Afterwards, he returned to the Primrose House, crossed the lobby, and approached the desk. The clerk, who he assumed was Mr. Selby, was doing some paperwork in a cubbyhole beside the key rack, where he could keep an eye on the desk. At Sam's approach, he left his work and came up behind the desk.

Sam said, "I'm just guessing, but would you be Mr. Selby, the owner?"

"I am," the gray-faced owner replied. "Anything wrong, Mr. Kennery?"

"Nothing wrong. I'm after information. Where's the newspaper office?"

"Primrose hasn't got a newspaper, Mr. Kennery. We're too close to the *Capital Times* in Junction City."

"What do you do for local news? Pick it up at the barbershop?"

Mr. Selby smiled and said, "Partly, but the *Capital Times* prints the Primrose news. It gives us a whole page about three times a week."

"They've a correspondent here?"

Again Selby nodded. "Yes. He's a bright young fellow that clerks at Pollock's Emporium down the street. Name's Ben Harness."

Sam thanked him and went out. This was a chore he should have done in Junction City, but Wilbarth, understandably in a hurry to beat the trial date, had not given him time. He wanted to read the account of Schaeffer's murder and the indictment of Brayton and Herrington. Maybe it would answer some questions he hadn't had the time or the sense to ask Wilbarth.

Pollock's Emporium was a huge store that sold dry goods, hardware, and groceries. The hardware section was closest to the door through which Sam entered, and he inquired of the clerk where he could find Bill Harness.

The clerk pointed to a red-haired young man behind the adjoining dry goods counter, and Sam moved over there and halted before him.

"Something for you?" Harness asked. He had a bright, friendly face and couldn't have been over twenty.

"I'm Sam Kennery. Don't want to buy anything, but maybe you can help me. You're Primrose's correspondent for the *Capital Times*, I'm told."

The young man nodded and, at the same time, grimaced. "Yes, sir. The worst newspaper in the West, and I guess I help make it bad."

Sam grinned and the young man smiled too. "Do you keep a file of the *Times*?"

"I surely do," Harness answered wryly. "Why? Well, Red Macandy — he's the editor — is not only the crookedest newspaperman in the state, but the cheapest and the drunkenest. He pays me by the line for what I send him. Every month his check is short, so I keep a file to check against his swindling."

"Could I have a look at that file?"

"Help yourself," young Harness said. "It's in my room at Mrs. Blake's boardinghouse." He jerked his thumb over his shoulder. "That's a white-painted house on the right in the middle of the next block, right behind the store. Tell her I sent you." He hesitated.

"Or maybe I could remember what it is you want to look up?"

"Won't bother you with it. I'm much obliged for the look at your files."

The redhead nodded, then said, "They're stacked in my closet, the newest on top."

Out on the street, Sam followed Ben Harness's directions, found the house, and, as predicted, the door was opened by a buxom, gray-haired Mrs. Blake, who, after Sam stated his business, directed him to Harness's room, the last on the left of the upstairs corridor.

Harness's room was small; crowded, book-filled shelves almost covered one wall. The single easy chair and the made bed, along with a littered desk and a straight chair, jammed the room.

Sam threw his hat on the desk, then opened the closet. With both hands he lifted the top third of the two-foot pile of newspapers, placed it beside the easy chair, and then settled down for some reading.

The account of Brayton's and Herrington's arraignments was reported with bias, malice, and relish in the series of articles signed by Red Macandy. The bare facts were stated plainly enough. The charge against Brayton and Herrington was a dual one: collusive embezzlement and defrauding the United States Government of an excess of twenty thousand dollars. However, Macandy had not been content with the bare facts. Brayton, according to him, had been a failure in three businesses in the old territorial days, before Senator Wagenknecht had paid off a debt by wangling him a job as Indian agent. Macandy hinted that Brayton had used blackmail on the senator, who was a wenching and drinking companion of Brayton when they were both territorial legislators in the capital city. Brayton's wife had left him because of his fondness for the company of women other than herself. Macandy went into as much detail as he dared about the failure of Brayton's three businesses. Macandy's article barely skirted libel, and Sam guessed that Macandy could probably prove everything he wrote about Brayton. It was a cruel piece of writing, Sam reflected. After all, Ulysses S. Grant had failed in business and was overfond of the bottle, but he was quite a general.

In the following issue of the *Times*, Macandy took Herrington apart in a similar article. He had less to work on here, for Herrington was neither a native of the state nor a government official. Macandy had managed, however, to dredge up a half-dozen arrests of Herrington for disturbing the peace in a succession of trail towns. He hinted that the embezzlement of twenty thousand dollars was laughable, pointing out that the charge covered only three of the six years during which Brayton had been associated with Herrington. The true amount of the embezzlement was probably triple the sum the government named. Herrington, Macandy said, had got his nickname, "Big Dad," not because of his size, but because of the astounding number of progeny he had fathered in Texas while remaining a bachelor. Macandy was careful to say this was only one of the many rumors that seemed to follow Herrington, such as his infinite capacity for alcohol, his friendly spending, and his maniacal rages.

Attorneys for the two men were Amos Thurston and Lee Phelan of the firm of Thurston, Phelan & Russell, who were also the attorneys for the giant Consolidated Mining & Milling Company of Primrose.

Sam now hunted down the issue of the *Times* that had reported the ambushing of Morton Schaeffer. The only thing new that he learned from the account was Macandy's speculation that there had to be two ambushers, since how could a single man prowling around the Long Reach water tank in the darkness be certain on which side of the passenger car Morton would be seated? If he had chosen the wrong side, Macandy reasoned, he would either have had to ride around the locomotive, and thus risk being seen by the engine crew, or around the entire train. The shot had come too soon after the train had stopped for him to have done that; therefore, Macandy argued, there must have been two assassins, one on each side of the train.

Macandy pointed out, of course, that Schaeffer was the prosecution's star witness in the upcoming trial of Herrington and Brayton. By adding that Schaeffer had no other known enemies, he implied that Herrington and Brayton were the only ones who could profit by Schaeffer's death. He was, in fact, pointing the finger of suspicion at them while stating that both men had unimpeachable alibis at the time of Schaeffer's murder. He was right, Sam thought. Wilbarth and Newford had probably gone over the details of the ambush so many hundreds of times that they had forgotten to tell him of the probability that two men had staged the ambush.

The delays of the trial that the court had granted

were duly noted in subsequent issues of the *Times*.

When Sam was finished reading, he wondered what he had learned. Thanks to Red Macandy's poison pen, he had a pretty fair character assessment of the two conspirators. He knew he could never like this Red Macandy, but his guess was that Macandy's hints, innuendoes, and reports of rumors held a measure of truth. The other thing he had learned was that two men were probably involved in the murder of Morton Schaeffer.

Dusk was beginning to fall when Sam returned the papers to their pile and scribbled a note of thanks to Harness, which he propped against the pillow, and left the house.

Somehow, tonight if possible, he had to meet Herrington and be accepted by him. If Herrington accepted him, Brayton would too. Lacking any other way of meeting Big Dad, there was only the chance of an open poker game.

When he entered the Primrose House and turned toward the bar, he saw that it was beginning to fill up. Even before he reached the door, he heard, with an irritability rare in him, the bray of Herrington's laugh. Sam thought, *The rope'll choke that off, my fat friend.* The bar was fairly crowded, and all the chairs at both tables were taken up by cardplayers. Glancing at the rear table on his way to an empty place at the bar, Sam saw that Herrington had the same seat he had occupied at noon; Seeley Carnes, as before, sat on his right. All the chairs were filled and Sam knew he would have to wait until one of the players cashed in his chips.

The bartender recognized him and said, "Good

evening, Mr. Kennery. What's your pleasure?"

"That same whiskey," Sam told him. He wondered if Mr. Selby, the proprietor, made a point of instructing all his help, including his daughter, to learn the names of the hotel's guests. After all, he was a stranger in town some seven hours, and had already been called by his name several times by several people. Could it be that they knew of him and the purpose of his visit? That he decided, was impossible.

He poured his drink just as Herrington's bellowing laughter overrode the noisy talk of the room. Again Sam winced.

His drink down, he was thinking about another when he felt a hand grasp his elbow. He half-turned to confront a stocky bulldog of a man wearing the badge of a law officer on his open vest. He had a square, tough face that was unsmiling now. This would be Sheriff Morehead. Sam had a dismal feeling of impending disaster. *The damned idiot,* he thought. Wilbarth had said Morehead would get in touch with him, so Morehead had chosen to greet him in from of fifty men, including the man they were both after.

"Mister, I've had my eye on you," the sheriff said in a hoarse, gravelly voice.

Looking at him closely, Sam saw the wink of eye.

"Will you please come along with me to my office?"

Did the wink mean the sheriff wasn't serious? Sam didn't know, and he thought he might as well play this as any stranger would.

"What for? I like it here."

"I won't ask you again," the sheriff said. His voice

seemed to overpower other voices in the room, and talk trailed off.

Sam said quietly, "I said I like it here."

"Come along. I don't want trouble."

Sam said, loud enough so the whole room could hear it, "Go away."

The sheriff took one step backwards and his hand fell to his gun.

Swiftly, then, Sam's hand blurred to his holster and came up with his sixgun cocked and pointed.

A look of disbelief came into the sheriff's face, but his right hand moved outward away from his gun.

"That'll get you dead, Sheriff."

The men closest to the two began to back off, crowding into each other.

The sheriff stared at him for a long moment and then said, "You might's well come now. If I go away, I'll come back with three more men. They'll have shot guns."

Sam pretended a sullen indecision. "What do you want of me?"

"Nothing, but I think another sheriff does. Now, what'll it be? Shotguns?"

"I should have shot you," Sam said wryly, and begin to holster his gun.

Before his gun reached its holster, Morehead extended his hand. "I'll take that."

Grudgingly, Sam held out the gun and Morehead took it.

"Now walk out ahead of me through the lobby."

Sam moved past Morehead as talk began to swell. He wanted to look over to see if Herrington had watched this, but that was too risky. With a surly sneer on his face, eyes ahead, he tramped past the standing cardplayers, into the lobby, and out the veranda door. He could hear the excited talk well up behind him. On the boardwalk, Morehead caught up with him and they took a few strides side by side in silence.

"Pretty good for no rehearsal," Morehead said dryly. He looked sideways and up at Sam. "For a minute I thought I had the wrong man and I was dead."

"What's it get us?"

"We hate each other, for one thing."

"That was for Herrington, then?"

"Mostly."

Two men were approaching, and by the light of the veranda lamps, Sam saw them looking curiously at the sheriff and himself. Just as they were passing, Sam said, "You couldn't be dumber or wronger if you were drunk Sheriff."

The sheriff waited until the two men were out of earshot, then said quietly, "Keep it up. That's what we want."

At the sheriff's rear-corner office in the big stone courthouse a block behind the Primrose House, the sheriff turned up the lamp on his desk, closed the door, then gestured to a chair beside his rolltop desk. His office, Sam thought, could be duplicated in every county seat in the state — the littered desk, the gun rack on the wall, the ancient horsehair sofa for the wounded or the weary, the foul cuspidor for the chewers, and the recently received reward dodgers tacked to the wall.

Morehead slumped into the swivel chair in front of

the desk and regarded Sam carefully. Sam said nothing, knowing this was the first real look Morehead had had at him.

"Thought you'd be older," Morehead said.

Sam smiled faintly. "I'm beginning to think I've got a baby face."

Morehead shook his head. "It's not that, it's — doesn't matter." He tilted his chair back, cleared his throat, and said, "Met Herrington yet?" When Sam shook his head, Morehead said, "You will tonight."

"You sound pretty sure."

"I am," Morehead said flatly. "Any man that hates the law is Herrington's friend. He's been riding me and now he'll ride me more."

"Where's Brayton?"

"Due in tomorrow. He had to go back to the agent on some government business. I've got a deputy with him."

"Anything I should know about him?"

"I'll answer that question by asking you one," Morehead said and he almost smiled. "You got a good head for drink?"

"Average, I reckon. Why?"

"Brayton's never really sober, but don't let that fool you. He never makes a slip, so don't count on his booze helping you."

Sam nodded. Booze and women. Wilbarth had said. "What else can you tell me about either of them?"

Morehead sighed and shook his head. "Nothing. When they aren't drinking at the Primrose bar, they're drinking at one of the sporting houses across the river. They spend a lot of time with their lawyers. That's all

I can tell you after watching them for ten days."

"Do they ever talk about their trial?"

"Yes. They claim there won't be one," Morehead said sourly.

The sheriff rose. "I think you better go back now, Kennery. I've told you all I know, which is nothing. Your story is that I got a reward dodger today that fitted your description. One of the aliases of the wanted man was Kennedy. Kennery is close enough to that, plus the description, to make me pull you in for questioning. Your alibi is that you were in prison when Kennedy committed the crime. You showed me your prison release, which I'll keep until you leave town."

Sam grinned. "What was I in prison for?"

"Take your choice," the sheriff offered with grim humor.

Sam rose now. "You're not telling me to move along or to stay here, are you?"

"No, you're a free man, but bad, and I'll be watching you, tell them."

"But will they ask?" Sam asked wryly.

"If they don't, I'll turn in my badge," Morehead said in his gravel voice. He extended his hand. "Good luck. If I can help, let me know."

On his way back to the Primrose House, Sam thought about Morehead's move tonight. It was a clever one. If Morehead was right, it was the best of all possible ways to gain an introduction to Herrington —but once he'd met him, where did he go from there? Again he didn't know, and the only thing he could do was wait for the mistake that Herrington or Brayton had to make. As he mounted the veranda steps, he weighed his next move. Should he go into the bar and brag, or should he do what the average hardcase, familiar with trouble, would do? The latter course seemed the most sensible, and when he entered the lobby, he crossed it, heading for the dining room.

Louise Selby, standing by the door, gave him a cool nod of recognition, but just that. There was no smile, no small talk.

The dining room was not even half-full, and Sam headed for the table where he had been seated that noon. Herrington and Carnes were not in the room, and he supposed they were still drinking.

Tenney must have been in the kitchen, for Sam didn't see her. The menu blackboard told him, take it or leave it, that he was having steak for supper. At that moment, Tenney came out of the kitchen, saw him, hesitated only a second, then came up to his table. Her dark eyes were chill, and the smile was absent from her usually cheerful face. She halted beside him and said in a dull voice, "Good evening, sir."

Sam looked up at her, feeling a faint surprise. "The name is Sam Kennery."

"Yes, sir. Mr. Kennery."

"Make it Sam."

"No, Mr. Kennery."

Sam was silent for a moment, regarding her, and then he knew what was wrong. It was the same thing that had made Louise Selby greet him with the barest civility. He watched Tenney as she filled his glass.

"How would you like your steak, sir?"

"If I said rare you'd bring me charcoal. What's wrong, Tenney?"

"Who said anything was? And don't call me Tenney."

"That business with the sheriff?" Sam asked.

"Oh, that's nothing," Tenney said bitingly. "Somebody threatens to kill Sheriff Morehead every day. Mr. Selby encourages all our customers to do it."

"Nobody leans on me, Tenney. Not even if he wears a star."

"Why did he try to?"

"He thought I fitted the description on a reward dodger."

"And did you?"

Let's get it over with, Sam thought. "No, I was in prison when the crime the dodger named was committed."

Tenney looked swiftly at him obviously shocked, and then her glance slid away. "How would you like your steak, sir?"

"Rare, and don't bother putting arsenic in the gravy. I can tell."

"Rare, no arsenic," Tenney said evenly. She turned and headed for the kitchen.

This is one thing you hadn't counted on, my friend, Sam thought. *You can't be a hardcase in the eyes of the town and be a jolly good fellow to Tenney.* She was the town and saw what the town saw and heard what the town said. To her, then, he was a hardcase — too fast with a gun, bad-tempered, insanely rash, and a rebel with a prison record to boot. That was the character he had assumed for Herrington, and the one he must wear for Tenney.

When she returned with his supper, she placed his plate before him and said tonelessly, "Would you like coffee, Mr. J.B.?"

Sam looked up at her and saw that her face was cold with anger.

"J.B. standing for what?" he asked.

"Jailbird, sir," Tenney said, and moved off, heading for the kitchen again.

Sam's perception told him that she cared enough about their new and day-old relationship to be disappointed, angry, and contemptuous because of his revelation. If he had been just another man to her, she wouldn't have bothered to get angry, and that thought comforted him a little. Neither of them spoke when she returned with his coffee and left again.

Finished with his supper, Sam paid at the desk and Louise Selby unsmilingly gave him his change and thanked him. Like Tenney, she did not want to look at him and spoke her civil good night with eyes averted. As he stepped into the lobby, he heard Herrington's bray of laughter coming from inside the saloon. He halted now, mentally rehearsing his next move. The thing to do was act as if nothing out of the ordinary had happened, which in itself would suggest that he had done this before and that he regarded the sheriff as a bumbling fool who just happened to wear a star.

Sam turned and saw Mr. Selby approaching across the carpet. He waited until the gray-faced little man halted before him.

"I'm told you drew a gun on Sheriff Morehead, Mr. Kennery. Is that correct?"

"It is." Sam paused, watching him. "Do you want me to leave?"

"I've been thinking of asking you to, but I decided against it. I just want you to understand that shooting or fighting in my saloon won't be tolerated. Alec has a shotgun under the bar that he's not afraid to use."

"Has there been any shooting or fighting, Mr. Selby?"

"No, and there'd better not be."

"Who went for his gun first?" Sam asked quietly.

"The sheriff, and he has a right to."

"You're wrong there, but I won't make trouble for you, Mr. Selby."

Sam saw the look of righteous contempt in the hotel owner's eyes before he turned and moved toward the saloon.

The room was fairly crowded, and Sam, after a casual glance around the room, had to make his way toward the rear of the room before he could find a slot for himself at the bar. In his search for a space, he had seen Herrington and Carnes seated at their usual table.

Alec, the bartender, came up to him, but this time there was no greeting. Wordlessly he placed a bottle of Sam's favorite whiskey and a glass on the bar and retreated. Sam was, of course, in Alec's bad books too.

He poured a drink he really didn't want, and looked up into the backbar mirror and could see only the bar drinkers toward the front of the room reflected in it. He was suddenly aware that the talk had muted, and he saw that he was being watched by several of the saloon patrons. He was reaching for his glass when a deep voice behind him said, "My friend, I'd like to introduce myself." Sam turned slowly and saw Herrington, a smile under his beak of a nose, his hand extended.

"I'd like to shake your hand, Kennery. My name's Herrington."

Sam extended his hand, a calculated look of puzzlement on his face.

"Mr. Herrington, how are you, sir?"

"Like to join us for a drink? It's a pleasure to meet the man that made Morehouse take water."

The corner of Sam's mouth lifted in a faint smile. "That's an easy way to earn a drink, Mr. Herrington."

"If you have the nerve," Herrington conceded. "Come along."

Seeley Carnes, wearing his hat as usual, rose at their approach, and Herrington introduced Sam and Carnes to each other. Sam sat down across from Carnes and put his hat on an empty chair next to him. Herrington eased his vast bulk into his chair and looked with approval at Sam, while Carnes poured the drinks.

"That showdown made my day, my week, my month," Herrington said, then opened his mouth and brayed his booming laugh.

Sam shrugged. "Somebody had to teach him some manners."

"What was graveling him? I saw it, but didn't hear anything."

"He wanted me to come with him and wouldn't tell me why. When I told him to go away, he started for his gun and I was ahead of him."

"By a Texas mile," Carnes said. He had a thin nasal drawl that Sam knew was going to bother him as much as Herrington's laugh.

"You went, though?" Herrington said.

Sam nodded. "He promised me three men with shotguns if I didn't."

Herrington looked at him shrewdly. "That means you want to stay here. If you didn't want to, you'd have shot him and run."

Sam nodded. "That's right. A man is going to meet me here."

"So you promised the sheriff you'd be a good boy, is that it?"

Sam grinned crookedly.

Seeley Carnes asked then, "Why'd he want you in the first place? You only came this morning."

Sam replied almost indifferently. "That's a standard play with some of these whistle-stop sheriffs. They spot a stranger they think means trouble, so they pull him in and question him. Sort of puts a man on notice that he's being watched, I reckon. Like a warning."

"What was his excuse for pulling you in? Like I said, I couldn't hear."

Sam grimaced in disgust. "The oldest one of all. He had a reward dodger that fitted my description." He paused, and then laughed. "The smart lawmen never figure this, but a man can change his looks at the nearest barbershop and change his name when he walks out."

Herrington's bray of laughter exploded, but Seeley regarded Sam unsmilingly.

"Was it you?" Carnes asked.

"Not this time," Sam said idly, then added, "The

wanted man was left-handed, the dodger said. All the sheriff had to do was look at where I wore my gun. Besides that, I was in jail when the crime was committed. No, the sheriff just wanted to warn me. I don't reckon he'd even read the dodger."

Carnes made no comment, and it occurred to Sam that Carnes was the shrewder of the two, even though he worked for Herrington. Carnes had picked up the fact that Sam had been here only one day, and his questions, though casual, were to the point.

"Well, I invited you over for a drink," Herrington said. "Pour 'em Seeley."

Carnes almost filled three big water glasses with whiskey and distributed the drinks. Sam picked up his glass, dipped his head to Herrington in a careless gesture of thanks, and the three of them drank. From his vest Herrington took out two cigars, tossed one to Sam, and put the other in his mouth and lighted it. Sam was wondering why Carnes hadn't been offered a cigar when Carnes reached in his pocket and drew out a doe-skin pouch. Then he lifted out a book of cigarette papers and extracted one. Opening the pouch, he lifted out the coarsest, blackest shreds of tobacco Sam had ever seen, rolled a cigarette, and lighted it. The first whiff of smoke from the cigarette hit Sam almost as a physical shock. It was the rawest, rankest reek of tobacco he had ever smelled, and it somehow reminded him of burning rope.

Sam fired up his cigar now, and surprised Herrington by regarding him carefully. Sam thought it was time for him to show a proper but polite curiosity. "You must be from around here."

Herrington shook his head. "How do you figure that?"

Sam shrugged. "You know the sheriff good enough to cuss him out."

Herrington looked at Seeley and Seeley said tonelessly, "Tell him, Dad."

Herrington regarded Sam with a look of pride and benevolence. "Kennery, if I had any hair, Sheriff Morehead would be in it. He greets us in the morning, checks on us at noon, and sees us to bed. You see, I'm waiting a court trial and Seeley's been subpoenaed as a witness."

Sam raised his eyebrows in feigned surprise, but he kept silent.

Herrington continued, "I'm a drover, Kennery, and Seeley here is my trail boss. We've been delivering contract beef to the agency up north for half a dozen years. Never had a complaint from the agent, but one of the agency's hired hands got a notion I was being paid for more cattle than I delivered." He took a gulp of whiskey and continued, "He said I split the overpayment with the agent, so me and the agent are charged with fraud. Trial's coming up in a week or so unless we can haze the judge into making it sooner."

Sam held up his cigar, studied it a moment, then looked over it at Herrington. "I've heard of a lot of long counts on Indian beef, but I never heard of a man going to jail for it." He scowled. "Your trial here?"

"Junction City," Herrington said, then added, "But there won't be any trial. The government's chief witness is dead, and they can't prove a thing without him. We're down here because the marshal in Junction City wouldn't let us alone. We got a court order restraining him from — they call it 'harassment,' don't they?''

"I wouldn't know," Sam said. "They got the agent locked up?"

"We're both out on bond," Herrington said sourly. "He had to go back to the agency with the guard Morehead put on him. He'll be in tomorrow."

Sam said philosophically, "They never let a man alone, do they?"

"It's a damned nuisance," Herrington growled. "Pour up, Seeley, then we better go eat before they lock the dining room on us."

Seeley poured another big drink for each of them, and Herrington downed his in two huge gulps. Seeley did the same, but Sam only took a sip of his.

Now Herrington rose. "Come and eat with us, Kennery."

"I've had supper, thanks."

"Well, come and sit with us."

"That fellow I was supposed to meet, remember?" Sam said. "He might come in."

"Hell, he'll check at the desk."

Sam said quietly, "He won't know me by that name," and grinned.

Herrington smiled knowingly. "See you later, then."

Seeley Carnes gave him only a curt nod before he picked up their bottle and they made their way out of the bar.

Well, Morehead knew his men, Sam thought. Herrington had made the move the sheriff had anticipated.

Sam's story had seemed to convince Herrington and Seeley both, although Sam wondered about Seeley. Was he really convinced that Sam was what he pretended to be? Behind that poker face and those chill eyes, was there a suspicion of him? Hadn't it been Seeley, though, who urged Herrington to tell of the fraud? Was there a purpose behind his urging, or was it his stiff way of acknowledging that they too were crooked, and proud of it?

Sam looked with distaste at the glass of whiskey before him. It wouldn't do to leave it here for them to find on their return; that was bad saloon manners. Yet he didn't want the drink. He reached out for the glass, cupped it in his hands for a moment, then unobtrusively poured the contents in the cuspidor beside his chair.

Afterwards he went up to his room.

Three

Herrington and Carnes were greeted at the dining room door by a distant and resigned Louise Selby. She gave them a cool good evening and let them find the way to their usual table. They had come in just as she was about to close the doors, which meant that one of the girls, and probably Mrs. Payne, would have to stay late to take care of their suppers.

Big Dad led the way to their table, where Seeley took off his hat, put the bottle on the table, and sat down across from his boss. Mary, the plump waitress, came up to their table, filled their glasses with water, and took their orders. The first thing both men did was to drink half the water in their glasses and refill them with whiskey. It was a practice Louise Selby loathed, but her father had told her to ignore this dining room drinking, since they were good spenders and had caused no trouble so far.

"What do you think of this Kennery?" Big Dad asked.

"Well, he's got nerve all right," Carnes conceded.

Herrington looked at him shrewdly. "What's there about him you don't like, Seeley?"

Carnes' thin lips curled up at the corners. "Well, for one thing, he ain't from Texas."

"Besides that, though?"

"He talks too good."

"Like me, you mean?" Big Dad said. "Hell, if they teach you to read, you can't help but talk different."

"I reckon," Carnes said indifferently.

"You think he's a real hardcase, Seeley?"

"Gamblin' type, maybe." Seeley frowned. "He ain't duded up like a dealer. Still, he's got money and he don't ask about jobs. He can unload with a gun too. Yeah, I'd say he's a hardcase, but only medium hard."

Herrington took a swig of his drink, and looked reflectively over Carnes' head. "He's what I was fifteen years ago, before I got me this belly. You didn't know me then, did you, Seeley?"

"No, but I'd sure as hell heard of you."

"Wonder if he'll be around after the trial?" Herrington asked.

Seeley drank, then wiped his mouth with the back of his hand and said, "Dunno. Why do you care?"

"I'd like to have him around," Herrington said. "He makes me laugh, and I figure he'll fight for money, marbles, or chalk, just for the hell of it."

"What would he do?"

Herrington shrugged his massive shoulders. "Segundo to you, during the winter. Buy cattle, trade for horses, but mostly take on any Y.S. rider he meets, even hunt 'em."

Mary brought their food then, and while they ate in silence, Seeley reflected on what his boss had said. Kennery would work under him in the winter and probably take a trail herd north next summer. True, he might be of help in Big Dad's long-standing and continuing feud with Yancey Slater and his crew. For the past five years, Big Dad had hired every one of his Chain Link hands with the utmost care. First they must know how to handle a gun and when to use it. Their willingness and ability to work, he left up to Seeley to develop. What Big Dad wanted was a mean, tough, fighting, hair-trigger crew that could steal far more beef than was stolen from them. Kennery fitted the requirements, but was there something beyond that? To put Kennery in as segundo meant that Dad would have to demote Harry Olds, who would quit, and jump Kennery over four or five fight- and trail-hardened hands who wouldn't take kindly to the move. It would mean that Big Dad wanted to groom Kennery for his own job of foreman and trail boss.

It could happen, Carnes thought cynically, remembering how he himself had been hired ten years ago when he was twenty. He and a colored cowboy were driving a remuda south, and stopped off at Tascosa for a drink and some sleep, and the Chain Link bunch was passing through too. Typically, they were cocky, quarrelsome, and mean. Seeley and his colored partner were in no mood for the hazing the Chain Link crew tried to give them. Gunplay broke out in the saloon and Seeley, quick with a gun, killed their chief tormenter and wounded two others before he made it across the street to the shelter of a feed barn. About eight of them came after him, surrounded the barn, and started moving in on him. He was alone, for his partner lay dead on the saloon floor. His chances of surviving this one were next to nothing, he reckoned. They would get him in the end, but he would take a couple more with him.

It was then that **Big Dad Herrington**, known all over the Panhandle and below it for his fighting, feuding, and hell-raising, stepped through the saloon doors onto the boardwalk. Seeley knew who he was, and had already decided to go for the chief and forget the Indians, when Herrington bellowed to his men. Singly and in pairs, under a blasting sun, they came over to him. Seeley thought, *Well, I can't be this lucky,* and waited. After a short parley, the Chain Link crew moved back into the saloon, leaving Herrington standing alone. Then Herrington started toward the feed barn. Even then he was a bear of a man, short-legged but tall, without the belly he toted around now. He stopped in the door of the feed barn and called, "Come out, you. The shootin's over."

Seeley, covering Herrington, came out from behind a feed box. Herrington moved into the shade and the two men halted, regarding each other.

"Who you working for?" Herrington asked.

"Myself. Trading horses."

"Stealing them too?" Herrington continued, still amiable.

"When I can," Seeley answered calmly.

Herrington laughed then. It was the first of ten thousand of those braying laughs that Seeley was to hear, and he hadn't liked it any better then than he liked it now.

"Well, I'll buy your horses and you'll work for me," Herrington said.

"How do you know I want to?"

"Well, figure it out," Herrington said. "I can call those boys back, and more with 'em."

"And I can shoot you before you even start across the street."

Herrington laughed again. "I like that. Sure you could, but you won't. You'll take my offer."

"Hell, your crew would shoot me the first time I turned my back."

"Not if I say no, and I've already said no. They started that trouble and they paid for it. There'll be no grudges, and you better not carry one, either. Now come along."

This was the way Big Dad had hired him, and it was because he was outnumbered and had chosen to fight rather than take water. And this could be the way he would hire Kennery, who had backed Sheriff Morehead down. Seeley liked Big Dad and was loyal to him, but he had no illusions. Over these ten years, Seeley had learned that when caution took the place of daring, when thought replaced action in a man, he was useless to Big Dad. Well, Herrington couldn't fault Seeley on that score, and Seeley intended that he never would.

Seeley said aloud now, "Yes, he could give Yancey's boys some trouble, but can you get him?"

"I'll find a way," Big Dad said quietly, and reached for his whiskey glass.

The next morning, Herrington and Carnes were numbered in the small group that waited on the depot platform as the train from Junction City pulled in. It was a crisp morning, sunny and almost chill. As the passengers filed off, a tall, emaciated man in a dark townsman's suit cut away from the other passengers and moved toward Herrington and Carnes in a long, ungainly, almost impatient stride. When Con Brayton halted before the other two, he did not offer to shake hands and neither did they, nor did he bother to put down his carpet-covered valise.

"Well, Con, where's nursie?" Herrington asked.

"I left him asleep in the seat," Brayton said contemptuously. "He couldn't guard a ten-day-old baby."

Herrington's bray of a laugh came then, and Brayton eyed him almost balefully, as if he had learned to live with Herrington's laugh but didn't like it. His white shirt and string tie, along with his black Stetson, gave him a vague air of authority, as if he might be a preacher or a doctor. In spite of his height, he was a stoop-shouldered man with a long, creased, drink-ravaged face. Full black mustaches managed to hide a weak mouth, but only emphasized a receding chin above a huge Adam's apple. His gray, red-rimmed eyes were arrogant with meanness. He said impatiently, "If we want a seat in the hack, we'd better move."

The three men turned and moved toward the hack at the edge of the platform.

"How's your Injuns, Con?"

"Stinking. As usual."

Because of the presence of other passengers in the hack, they did not speak on their short ride to the Primrose House. Once in its lobby, Herrington said, "Dump your bag and we'll meet you in the saloon."

"No, come up to the room," Brayton said flatly. "We've got to talk. I got a bottle."

"Full?" Herrington asked.

"No. Seeley, pick up a bottle and some glasses in the bar, and then come up."

Brayton went over to the desk, picked up his key from Mr. Selby, and then led the way up the stairs. Once in his room, while Herrington crossed it and looked out the window, Brayton shucked out of his coat, loosened his tie, then took a bottle from his bag.

Without turning, Herrington said, "What's bothering you, Con?"

"Wait for Seeley." Brayton said curtly.

Herrington turned now, and was thoughtful as he watched Brayton, bottle in hand, cross to the washstand, pour a couple of inches of whiskey in a tumbler, and toss it down. The door opened then, and Seeley came in carrying a tray with a bottle and three glasses.

Brayton said, "Make your own," and crossed over to the bed and sat on the edge of it. Herrington moved away from the window now, and on his way to the bottle, he handed Brayton a cigar, which Brayton accepted with a grunt. While Seeley made the two drinks, Brayton fired up, and afterwards, as if it were his prerogative, Herrington came back to the room's single easy chair and sat down. Seeley, wearing his hat, put his shoulder against the wall by the washstand, rolled one of his stinking cigarettes, and waited for Brayton to begin.

Brayton looked at Herrington and said, "Dad, I think we got trouble."

"Up there? What kind?"

"Indian trouble. Specifically, Joe Potatoes."

"Hell, if he wants money, give it to him," Herrington said.

Brayton gave him a humorless smile, revealing big yellow-stained teeth below his mustaches. "That I've already done," he said dryly.

"Then what does he want?"

"*More* money. Lots more. It's what he's apt to do if he don't get it that scares me," Brayton said. "He and Lil — that's his wife — drank up what we paid him. It was more money than they'd had in their lives, and Lil likes it."

"I thought she was one of your girls, Con," Herrington said.

Brayton scowled. "What's that got to do with it? She still is, but she and Joe want money. They've got a taste for high living now."

Herrington's laughter was predictable. "High living," he said then. "A stinking sod hut with a couple of elk hides on a dirt floor — that's what they've got now. What do they want us to do? Build them a frame house?"

Brayton said wearily, "You don't get me, Dad. Up to now they've been too poor to buy booze steady. Now they've got a taste for it."

Seeley put in then, "Is Joe talking?"

Brayton shook his bead. "Not yet, but he says he will."

"Does Lil know about Schaeffer?" Seeley asked.

"Joe says no. These bucks tell their women only what they want to. All Lil knows is that Joe came up with booze money once, so why doesn't he do it again?"

"Why doesn't he throw her out?"

"Why, Joe feels like she does. He got money once, so he wants more."

The three men were quiet for a moment, and then Seeley Carnes broke the silence. "Kill him."

Brayton swiveled his head to regard him. "Who does it, Seeley? You, with one of Morehead's guards watching? Or me? Or Dad here?"

Seeley's lean face flushed. "No, I don't reckon."

"When the court frees me, I go back to the agency," Brayton said angrily. "You two go back to Texas. I got to live alongside of Joe and pay and pay and pay."

Seeley smiled thinly. "Wait until the court frees us all, and Morehead's guards are pulled off. I'll take care of him."

"It won't wait, Seeley," Brayton said flatly. "Joe gave me until the half-moon. That's a week."

Seeley swore viciously and pushed away from the wall. Looking at Herrington, he said, "That ain't enough time to send for anyone. Dad."

Herrington said one word: "Kennery."

Brayton looked at him and then at Seeley. Herrington and Seeley were looking at each other, ignoring him.

"What's going on here?" Brayton demanded "What's Kennery?"

"Sam Kennery," Herrington said quietly. "A hardcase that drifted in here on yesterday's train. Morehead tried to hoo-raw him and Kennery put a gun on him so fast you couldn't see his hand move. He's tough and mean and he's known jail. Known it a lot of times, I'd reckon."

"*He* says," Seeley said thinly.

Herrington scowled. "You don't trust him?"

Seeley shook his head. "I never said that. We just don't know him that good."

"Tell me more about him," Con said with sudden interest.

"All right, here's everything I know. Seeley, if I miss anything, tell me." Herrington went on, then, to describe their entire conversation with Kennery last evening, and Seeley listened critically, occasionally nodding confirmation to one or another of Dad's points. Brayton listened intently, but his face seemed to reflect a faint skepticism.

Herrington finished his account of the meeting by saying, "He's no tinhorn, Con. A tinhorn would have come back from the sheriff's office and bragged for a while in the saloon like he was saying, 'Look what I done. I'm a tough enough hombre that I backed down the sheriff.' Instead, you know what Kennery did after he left the sheriff's office?"

"Tell me."

"Went in and had supper alone, just like he figured nothing had happened — like if it did happen, it wasn't important. Like I told you, he even down-talked it to us." He looked at Carnes now. "I figure him for a cool head. What about you, Seeley?"

"If he didn't like you he could be trouble, all right," Seeley said, half grudgingly.

"If he's what you say he is, he'll likely come high," Brayton observed.

Herrington said with impatience, "What if he does? This way you only pay once, not every time Joe and

Lil feel like going on a drunk."

"How do you know he'll do it?"

"Damn it, man, I don't, but I'll bet my bottom dollar on one thing — if he turns us down, he won't run to the law with our proposition." He looked at Seeley. "Am I wrong?"

"I reckon you're right on that," Seeley drawled.

Now Herrington heaved his bulk out of the chair, crossed to the bottle, poured himself a drink, and moved over to Brayton, who had seated himself on the bed again. He replenished Brayton's drink, then came over and handed the bottle to Seeley, who poured his own.

Brayton drank, then wiped his lips with a swipe of his shirtsleeve. When he could breathe evenly he said, "Dad, you're asking me to trust a man I've never seen."

Herrington was standing before his chair, ready to sit down. He said, "Tell you what. Let's go down to the bar. My guess is Kennery will be there or will come there. Let's ask him to eat with us. You can see for yourself, Con. Look him over. Don't sound him out, just look him over."

"Fair enough," Brayton said. "Let's go."

Four

Sam, in his room, heard the three men in the corridor as they sought the stairs. He waited an impatient five minutes, and then moved out into the corridor himself and descended into the lobby. He cut across it and entered the barroom, which held a scattering of men dedicated to their noon drink.

As he approached the bar, he looked casually about the room, and saw Herrington and Seeley with a third man whose back was to him. None of them looked at him, so he didn't bother to wave, but moved up to the bar. Alec's greeting was civil but cool, as he put a bottle and a glass before Kennery. Since there was no change in Alec's attitude toward him, it was reasonable to suppose that he had gained no status in Alec's eyes by drinking with Herrington and Carnes. *A good man, this Alec,* Sam thought. *If you associate with crooks, then you're a crook too, in Alec's book.*

Sam poured a drink and had downed it when he saw Herrington's reflection in the bar mirror. Herrington was coming toward him, and Sam, not pretending surprise, turned to greet him. "Morning."

"And a good morning to you," Herrington said, extending his hand. Sam shook it and Herrington cupped Sam's elbow in his left hand in a friendly gesture. "Come on over to the table, Kennery. Want you to meet a fellow."

Sam nodded, turned, picked up his glass and bottle, and followed Herrington back to the rear table. Herrington gave Sam time to put his bottle and glass on the table, and, gave Brayton time to rise, before he introduced them. "Kennery, this is Con Brayton. He's the Indian agent I was telling you about last night."

Sam shook hands with Brayton, murmuring the amenities, while thinking that here was a scoundrel who really looked the part. As Sam and Brayton seated themselves, Herrington said, "What's the bottle for, Kennery?"

"It's my turn," Sam said easily. "Have a drink, gentlemen."

Although there was already a bottle on the table, Herrington politely accepted Sam's offer and was followed by the others.

Brayton said pleasantly, "Dad was telling me about your run-in with Morehead yesterday."

"Wouldn't call it a run-in." Sam said carelessly. Then he smiled. "It was more like a run-out by Morehead."

This brought a hoot of laughter from Herrington, and Sam reminded himself to make no more jokes, however sorry they were.

When Herrington's laughter ceased, Seeley Carnes asked, "Your friend show up, Kennery?"

"Not yet, but he's a fiddlefoot. Might even've met a girl. Still, he's bound to run out of money sometime."

"It's tough to find work around here now," Herrington said. "Roundup's over and the beef is shipped. There's a lot of men riding the grub line already. You can ask around, though."

"Not interested," Sam said. "He won't be, either."

Sam was aware that Brayton was covertly studying him, and now he looked at the agent surprising him into speech.

"You don't look like a miner, Mr. Kennery. Cattle and mining are all Primrose has to offer."

"We'll make out," Sam said carelessly, even smugly.

"You can always rob a bank," Herrington said, and laughed at his own joke.

Sam nodded and said unsmilingly, quietly, "If we have to, yes." He saw Herrington's quick glance at Brayton. Now he finished his drink.

"Dad, I'm hungry. Let's eat," Brayton said.

"On your money or government money?" Herrington asked, and winked at Sam.

Brayton gave his humorless, yellow-toothed smile. "They're the same thing, ain't they, Dad?"

They had finished their drinks by now, and Herrington said, "Come along, Kennery. You can't eat alone."

Sam nodded, rose, picked up his bottle, moved over to the bar, and silently paid Alec for the drinks. Remembering Brayton's close scrutiny of him, he wondered if there was any chance the agent might have heard of him and identified him. It was a remote chance, but if it were so, he'd know soon. He wasted a few moments in selecting some cigars, in order to give Brayton a chance to tell Herrington, in case the Indian agent had recognized him. Then he moved out into the lobby, and joined the three, and they moved into the dining room. They received a staged smile from Louise Selby, and moved through the room toward Herrington's usual table. Tenney, on her way with a tray to a diner near the door, saw them and moved around a table to avoid them. Sam, bringing up the rear, tried to catch her eye, but she looked straight ahead, ignoring him. To his encounter with Morehead and his confessed prison record, he was adding his association with Herrington, whom Tenney loathed. There was really no reason why she should speak, he thought grimly.

The noon meal turned out to be a kind of chess game for Sam, and a puzzling one. Brayton was trying, in a seemingly careless way, to find out his background and as much of his history as he could. Obviously, Sam couldn't hide the fact that he'd had some schooling, so he didn't try. His story was that he was the runaway son of a revivalist preacher, and had dedicated most of his short life to breaking every moral rule his father believed in. He'd been a trail hand, a bodyguard for a Mexican politician, a prospector, and a drifter. Without seeming to care much what he was revealing about himself, he invented a series of wry anecdotes about the scrapes he'd been in — shooting and non-shooting — that planted the information he wanted them to believe. Seeley Carnes, taciturn as usual, listened and watched and nodded, but took no part in the conversation.

It was a long meal, so long that they were the last ones out of the dining room and had to have the door unlocked for them by Louise Selby.

In the lobby, they halted and Brayton moved over

to where he could get a look at the clock behind the desk. Returning, he said, "We were due in the lawyer's office five minutes ago, Dad."

Herrington groaned. "Another two-hour session?"

"Longer, I reckon."

"Well, let's go by way of the bar." To Sam he said, "We'll see you around drinking time, Sam."

This was the first time Sam had been called anything but Kennery, and he was certain now that if Brayton had had any suspicions and had related them to Herrington before dinner, Herrington would not have called him by his Christian name. "Drinking time it is, Dad," Sam said carelessly.

The three of them headed for the bar, and Sam, remaining in the lobby, moved over to the desk, where a stack of the *Capital Times* was for sale. He bought a paper and then took a lobby chair where he could see through the glass doors into the dining room. Louise Selby, Tenney, and Mary were setting places for supper. Over his opened paper, Sam watched them. Presently, Louise appeared with Mary, who was carrying a coat. Louise let Mary and herself out and said goodbye to Mary, who crossed the lobby, heading for the veranda and the street. Louise disappeared down the corridor toward the Selby apartment, beyond the desk. All the help was accounted for, except Tenney, who would be in the kitchen.

Sam rose, and under the gaze of Mr. Selby, behind the desk, he moved toward the stairs and climbed them. The second-floor corridor was empty, and Sam turned left toward his own room. When he came to number eight he halted, tried the door, found it locked, then reached in his pocket for his key ring. He found the blank key of the same type as his own room key, and isolated it. Drawing a match from his pocket, he lighted it and held the blank over the flaming match until it was smoke-blackened. Then he inserted the blank key in the keyhole and twisted it firmly several times. Withdrawing the key, he noted where the lock tumbler had marked the smoke-blackened metal of the key. The key on the ring next to the blank was not really a key, but a heavy piece of wire. Putting this wire key against the blank, he drew out his pocket knife. Opening the longest blade, he scored the wire at the place opposite the mark on the blank. Then, isolating the wire from the other key, he slipped it into the blade slot of the knife, and using the knife as pliers, he bent the wire at the mark he had scored. Pocketing the knife, he inserted the wire into the keyhole, turned the wire, and heard the lock click open.

Stepping inside the room, he withdrew the wire key, closed the door behind him, and looked around. Although the two beds in Herrington's and Carnes' room had been made up that morning, the room was in a disarray that no chambermaid could do much about. A couple of saddles and saddle blankets were stacked in the corner behind the lone easy chair. Beside them were piled a couple of dozen issues of the daily *Capital Times*. Herrington and Carnes apparently kept close track of what the newspapers had to say about them. In the corner by the bed nearest the window was a bulky blanket roll, with a carbine leaning against it.

First he moved to the closet and saw that it held several suits, all of them of the size that would fit Big Dad. Several pairs of boots were lined up against the wall, and a small trunk was at the rear.

Moving to the dresser, he pulled open the top drawer, which held nothing but clean shirts and socks. He was lifting these when the door opened so silently he did not hear it. Then a voice said, "Well, jailbird, working your way back to prison?"

Before he looked, he knew it was Tenney speaking. When he glanced at her he saw her standing, her hand still on the doorknob, a look of anger mingled with contempt on her face.

He said levelly, "Come in and shut the door, Tenney."

"When I come in, I'll come with Mr. Selby. I watched you pick that lock from down the hall, and now you're caught."

"That's right," Sam said. He moved over to her, took her by the wrist, and firmly drew her into the room, saying, "Be quiet, Tenney." Then he shut the door. When he turned, he saw the fright in her face and saw her throat muscles begin to tighten for a scream. Swiftly, holding her by the shoulder, he clamped his free hand over her mouth, and in as gentle a voice as he could summon, he said, "Tenney! Tenney! Believe in me, will you?" He took the one hand from her mouth and the other from her shoulder.

"Believe in you!" Tenney said hotly. "You're nothing but a thief!"

"Tenney, we can't argue here." He pointed to the

easy chair. "Sit down in that chair and see if I steal anything."

"I will not."

"All right, stand there and watch me."

"You can't keep me here!" Tenney said fiercely.

"I don't want to keep you here," Sam said with strained patience. "All I want to do is search this room. Watch me do it."

He moved back to the dresser, checked the other drawers, then noted the copy of *Stockman's Journal*, on which shaving gear was laid out. Moving past the beds then, he moved over to Carnes' blanket roll. Throwing the carbine on the bed, he tossed the blanket roll beside it, then untied the thongs that held it. All the while, Tenney was watching him with suspicion and anger. When Sam glanced at her, he was not sure whether she would make a break for the door or not, but he was gambling on her curiosity.

Unrolling the blanket roll now, Sam saw the couple of shirts and two pairs of socks that seemed to comprise the only contents, except for a two-foot long twist of Carnes' favorite Mexican tobacco. This surprised him, because the roll had seemed much too heavy, when he had lifted it, to contain only these meager possessions. Parting the shirts, he saw that they had wrapped the two parts of a disassembled shotgun. He did not let the excitement he felt show in his voice as he looked across the room. "Come here, Tenney."

Slowly, Tenney moved over to him and Sam gestured toward the bared gun parts. Tenney looked at them, and then at him.

"It's a shotgun," Tenney said, and then added tartly, "If he had that rifle too, he had to carry it some where."

"That's right," Sam said quietly. He replaced the gun parts and the shirts, rolled up the blankets, tied them as they had been tied, stacked the blanket roll in the corner, and leaned the carbine against it just as he had found it.

"Let's go, Tenney."

"Yes. Right down to Mr. Selby."

"All right," Sam said agreeably. "But first we'll see your mother. Is she still in the kitchen?"

The strangeness of his question held Tenney silent for a moment, and then she said, "Yes. Why do you want to see her?"

"Is there a back stairs?" Sam asked. At Tenney's nod, he said, "Let's take that. Come along."

Once in the corridor, Sam took out his wire key, relocked the door, and fell in beside Tenney. They walked the length of the corridor in silence. At its end, Tenney opened the last door on the right and led the way down a dark stairwell only faintly lighted by a single window. The door at the bottom of the stairs opened into the kitchen, and Tenney opened it without so much as looking back at him.

It was a big kitchen, holding a long serving table in its center. A black iron range stood alongside a big sink with its pump. The serving table was flanked by several chairs, and at one of these chairs sat an attractive woman, so young-looking that she could have been Tenney's older sister. She wore a full apron over her half-sleeved blue cotton dress. She had been peeling potatoes, but when she saw Tenney followed by a man strange to her, she ceased her work. She looked at Tenney with puzzlement, then at Sam. In the level glance she gave him there was no friendliness, but neither was there fear. She had the look of a durable, patient woman who knew her worth.

Tenney moved around the table, and Sam, following, took off his hat. Halting by her mother, Tenney said, "Mother, this is Mr. Kennery. I was counting linen in the closet and heard him come upstairs. I watched him pick the lock of Mr. Herrington's room and I watched him search it."

Mrs. Payne looked at Sam again, this time more carefully, before she said, "Then go tell Mr. Selby."

"He wanted to see you first, Mother." Tenney looked at him contemptuously and added, "I don't know what for. Maybe he wants to buy me off, and thinks you'll let me take the money."

Mrs. Payne looked at Sam. "What do you want of me, Mr. Kennery?"

"Well, I wanted to meet the best cook I've ever known and I wanted to set a few things straight."

Mrs. Payne said unsmilingly, "What's there to set straight?"

"Plenty," Sam answered. "To begin with, Tenney started out liking me, and in two days she won't speak to me except when she catches me picking a lock."

"Maybe she doesn't think you have much character, Mr. Kennery. If you admit to picking a lock, she must be right."

"Is that what you think, Tenney?"

"That's too kind on you!" Tenney said hotly.

"You're nothing but a rough! You pulled a gun on Sheriff Morehead and you admit you've been in jail. You're even proud of it. You've cozied up to those three rotten men, and now I've caught you breaking into their room to see what you could steal!"

Sam nodded, and then did a strange thing. He was standing beside an empty chair. He raised his right foot, put it on the chair, reached inside his boot, and drew from a pocket sewn inside something he held hidden in his fist. Straightening up, he walked around the table and extended his fisted hand to Mrs. Payne. "Will you keep this for me, Mrs. Payne?"

Tenney's mother looked at him in bewilderment, then extended her hand. Sam deposited the badge of a deputy U.S. marshal in her palm. Both Tenney and her mother looked at it, and then, in mutual surprise, raised their glances to him.

"I'm a deputy U.S. marshal, Mrs. Payne. I'm on loan to the marshal's office at Junction City. You can confirm that by asking Sheriff Morehead."

"Be sure I will."

"I'm trying to hunt down the murderer of Morton Schaeffer. Does that name mean anything to you?"

"Nothing."

"He was to be the key government witness at the trial of Herrington and Brayton for criminal fraud. Do you recall a man being ambushed on a train at a water stop north of Junction City about a month ago?"

"I do, Mother," Tenney put in, sitting down slowly in a chair next to Mrs. Payne.

Sam didn't look at her. He was watching Mrs. Payne, who, in turn, was carefully regarding him.

"I'm here to find and arrest the man who used that shotgun," he continued.

"Then why did you hold a gun on Sheriff Morehead?"

"That was a fake, Mrs. Payne. It was Morehead's idea, and a clever one. I needed to meet Herrington and Brayton, because certainly Schaeffer's murder could profit only that pair. I had to prove I wasn't afraid of the law or impressed by it, and prove it in front of them. It's worked up to now, Mrs. Payne."

"Why are you telling me this?" Mrs. Payne asked.

"Because if you believe me, Tenney will believe me. And if Tenney believes me, she can help me."

Now he looked at Tenney, in whose face had appeared a flush of color.

"Are you saying I haven't a mind of my own?" she asked angrily.

"No. I'm saying I think you respect your mother's judgment. Am I wrong?"

Tenney's face softened. "No," she said quietly.

"Will you keep that badge for me, Mrs. Payne?"

"Why do you want me to?"

"I'll be traveling in some rough company," Sam said quietly. "If they found that on me, it would buy me a shot in the back." He paused. "Now do you believe me, Mrs. Payne?"

"I do," Tenney put in before her mother could speak. "Sam, was that shotgun I saw the one that killed Morton Schaeffer?"

"It could be, Tenney, but I'm not sure. Possession of a shotgun doesn't prove anything. We have to put Carnes with that shotgun at the Long Reach water tank on the night of September the thirteenth."

"How will you do that?" Mrs. Payne asked.

"That's where Tenney comes in, Mrs. Payne." To Tenney he said, "Can you get a look at the register in the lobby without making Mr. Selby suspicious?"

"Of course," Tenney said. "Mary and I look at it a lot. Mr. Selby wants us to learn and memorize the names of all the guests. So we're looking at it all the time."

"Can you find out what date Carnes signed in? Or maybe you remember?"

Tenney frowned and thought for a minute. "He came after Herrington and Brayton, but I really didn't notice when, Sam. There were usually one or two men with them at every meal. It wasn't until several days after he got here that I realized he was a regular." She stood up now. "I'll go look."

Tenney moved through the swinging doors into the dining room. Sam and Mrs. Payne regarded each other calmly now. Oddly, neither of them was ill at ease.

Sam said, "I've given Tenney a rough time, I'm afraid."

"She enjoyed your teasing, but the business with the sheriff frightened her."

Sam nodded. "It was meant to. I had a story to set up, and Tenney had to believe it and spread it."

Mrs. Payne smiled faintly. "Well, she believed it and spread it to me."

"Where it stopped, I'll bet."

"Yes. You see, I couldn't gossip if I wanted to. The Selbys and the girls are the only people I see."

"You take Sundays off, don't you?"

73

She nodded. "Tenney takes over here and I ride all day, mostly to get the kitchen smell out of my head."

"If I'm here next Sunday, can I ride with you?"

Surprise came into Mrs. Payne's face. "Why, of course, but why would you want to?"

"I'm just guessing, but I think you need a man around you some of the time. I think you need to hear him, and cuss and scold him, or tell him how different things were when you were a girl."

Mrs. Payne's smile was a sad one, somehow acknowledging the truth of what Sam said. "It is lonely sometimes." She nodded toward the door in the rear wall. "We have two rooms back there. Counting them and the kitchen, that makes up our world."

"Tenney's, too?"

"No. Tenney has her good times. She goes to dances and church doings."

"With anyone special?" Sam asked carelessly.

Suddenly Mrs. Payne laughed, and Sam thought it was a pure delight to hear her.

He smiled and said, "Did I say something funny?"

"No, but you're making your point about my need to be around men."

Sam said, "You've lost me, Mrs. Payne."

"No I haven't. You like Tenney. You want to know if she likes you or if she likes some other man. You've noticed the ring on her finger and you're wondering if she's engaged. I can tell you right now, her ring is only insurance against the attentions of drummers and cowboys. You'd be surprised how often it works." She paused. "How am I doing in my study of men?"

"You're doing all right in your study of this one," Sam said.

Tenney came back from the dining room and found them laughing. She was so surprised that she halted, looking from one to the other, and said, "What are you two laughing at?"

Sam looked at Mrs. Payne and said quietly, "I think your mother will tell you sometime, Tenney. What did you find out?"

Tenney came over and sat down once again in the chair she had vacated. "Seeley Carnes registered on September fifteenth, Sam. Does that mean anything?"

Sam was silent for a long moment, feeling a stir of excitement. "It could, Tenney. The trial was set for the fifteenth. Schaeffer was killed on the thirteenth. It's a long two days' ride from the Long Reach water tank to Primrose, but it could be done." He shook his head. "Still, suspicion isn't proof."

He stood up. "Tenney, how has Carnes treated you?"

"Why, not at all. When I had their table, he never spoke to me except to order. I'd guess he hadn't even noticed that Mary's waiting on him and I'm not."

Remembering Mary's dumpy figure, Sam said dryly, "Your guess is wrong. Still, keep it that way, Tenney. You don't like Herrington, so you don't like Carnes. Treat him like you've been treating me, and keep on treating me the same way." He reached for his hat and said, "Thank you both."

The two women watched him cross the kitchen and take the back stairs, closing the door behind him.

Tenney picked up her apron, tied it, and sat down.

Mrs. Payne was already at her task of peeling the potatoes, and when Tenney picked up her knife and reached for a potato, Mrs. Payne said quietly, "Say something, Tenney."

"All right. I'm numb."

"You're not alone," her mother said.

Sam climbed to the second floor, his mind still turning over the information Tenney had gotten for him. Of the three men, Seeley Carnes would be the hardest to get close to. Beyond that, there were still things that Sam couldn't answer. How did Seeley know the Primrose & Northern stopped at the long Reach water tank, and that it would be dark? Brayton would know that, but Brayton was in Primrose with Herrington when Schaeffer was killed. Had Brayton made a previous trip to the agency — one Sam didn't know about? If he had, he could have met Carnes and briefed him, or the second killer could have known the train time, but who was he? It was important that he see Morehead tonight, and try to sort out the pieces of this puzzle. He would also have to tell him of the Payne women's knowledge of his identity. Had he been foolish in trusting Tenney and her mother? He didn't think he was that bad a judge of character. Tenney wouldn't gossip about him any more than her mother would, he was certain.

Five

Herrington, Brayton, and Carnes, as Big Dad had promised, were free of their lawyers by drinking time. They had saved a seat for Sam at what was turning out to be their private table in the crowded bar. Both Big Dad and Brayton seemed in low spirits, while Carnes was his usual taciturn self. Over whiskey, Sam learned that their lawyers had failed again to win a dismissal of their case by the court. The prosecution had been granted another week's postponement of the trial, and while Herrington and Brayton cursed the judge for a biased fool, Sam silently blessed him.

Both Brayton and Herrington drank heavily before and during supper, and Sam looked forward with dread to a long and alcoholic evening in their company. At supper he kept glancing covertly at Tenney, who, as far as he could tell, never once looked at him. He had a mounting feeling that this situation with his three companions was becoming intolerable. True, he had forged a tenuous link between Seeley Carnes and Schaeffer's murder, but the proof of it must come from one of the three. The initiative was in their hands; all he could do was listen passively, hoping that an incautious word, a slip of the tongue, would betray them.

Sam heard his name spoken, and looked up to find all three men regarding him curiously.

"The whiskey gettin' to you, Sam?" Herrington

asked from across the table. "I've been talkin' to you and you never heard. You comin' down drunk?"

Sam grinned faintly and shook his head. "No, I was just thinking, Dad. This fellow I was to meet was due here ahead of me. I've been here two days now, and there's been no sign of him and no word from him. I was studying on what might have happened to him, is all. What were you saying to me?"

"I said, why don't we all go up to my room where we can talk private?"

"Suits me," Sam said indifferently.

They rose, paid at the door, and then mounted the stairs to Herrington's and Carnes' room. Sam entered the room after Big Dad, and looked about it casually, as any man does when he enters a strange room. There were new papers on the dresser top, which they had probably brought back from their lawyer. While Seeley got Brayton's key and went next door for an extra chair, Herrington busied himself with pouring fresh drinks. When Seeley returned with the chair, he indicated that it was Sam's. Herrington took the easy chair, while Brayton and Seeley sat on separate beds. Herrington and Brayton fired up cigars, while Carnes built a cigarette and lighted the foul Mexican tobacco. Sam declined Herrington's offer of a cigar by saying, "No, I've had too many, Dad. A few more, and the first fresh air I breathe will knock me cold."

Herrington's laughter sawed at Sam's nerves, and he saw Herrington and Brayton exchange a glance.

"You want some fresh air, Sam?" Herrington asked quietly.

Sam grinned faintly. "You got any, Dad?"

Herrington smiled for once, instead of laughing. "Not here, but I can send you where there is some."

Sam came alert now, and a puzzled frown appeared on his face. He looked at the other two, who were now watching him intently, and then his glance returned to Herrington. "You trying to tell me something, Dad?"

Herrington nodded. "Kind of roundabout, Sam. We've got a job for you, if you'll take it."

"Outdoor job?"

"Outdoor job," Herrington confirmed, "Up north, on the reservation."

Sam scowled as he asked, "Doing what?"

Now Brayton took over. "Sam, I got me a trouble-making Indian up there. I want you to hunt him up and take him up in the mountains with about six quarts of whiskey. Don't bother feeding him, because he'll be so drunk he won't eat. When he's passed out for the tenth time or so, just take his clothes, his blankets, and his flint and steel. Pneumonia will do the rest, I reckon."

Sam studied the drink he was cradling in his lap, hiding his face in order not to betray, by his expression, the elation he felt. When he looked up, he saw the three men still watching him closely.

"With what kind of money, Con?" Sam asked calmly.

Herrington and Brayton exchanged glances, and Herrington said afterwards, "Would a couple hundred dollars do it, Sam?"

"You don't like this Indian, either, Dad?"

"That's right."

Sam nodded. "Yes, a couple hundred would do.

I've killed Indians for nothing."

Once more, Herrington's laugh exploded, and Sam waited until it died before asking Brayton. "Why this business with six quarts of whiskey, Con? Why don't I just give him a bottle to toll him out of camp, and then shoot him?"

"Yes, you can do that, but only if the other don't work."

"You just want him dead, is that it?"

Con nodded slowly.

Sam rose and went over to the bottle of whiskey on the desk. This Indian they wanted dead had to be either the ambusher or his partner. He must try to confirm this without seeming too curious. Picking up the bottle, he made the rounds, pouring each of them a drink and finally himself. All this time he kept silent. When he returned to his chair and sat down, Herrington said, "Something troubling you, Sam?"

Sam nodded. "A few things, Dad. Like who do I pull down on my head when I've killed him? Fifty Indians? The whole damn reservation? The U.S. Army or the U.S. marshal? Just so I know."

Brayton snorted. "Nobody, Sam. Oh, his wife will yell some, but she'll never know why he was killed or died."

"Can I be the judge of that, Con? Why am I killing him?"

Con and Herrington looked at each other and Sam thought, *Here it is.*

Now Seeley Carnes spoke for the first time, a single syllable. "No." He was answering Sam's question.

Both men looked at Seeley Carnes, and Sam tried

to read their expressions. Brayton looked annoyed and Herrington almost angry.

Herrington said impatiently, "We'll all be in this together after he's dead. What's the harm, Seeley? We got to have it done, don't we?"

"There's other men that'll do it," Seeley said.

Brayton grimaced in disgust. "You find one before the time's up, Seeley."

Seeley said nothing, only shrugged.

Sam put in quietly, "Maybe you better get yourselves a new boy. If you won't tell me what this will draw down on me, it must be plenty."

Brayton rose, with fury in his ravaged face. "God damn it, Seeley! You gone crazy?" He hesitated. "Come out in the hall." He headed for the door, and Seeley, after getting Herrington's nod, followed him.

Closing the door behind him, Seeley moved across the hall to where Brayton had halted.

"What the hell's the matter with you, Seeley? Kennery's already agreed to kill him. What's the matter with telling him why? Would you take money to kill a man when you didn't know what it would pull down on you?"

Carnes said in a flinty voice, "If I asked that question, I reckon the answer would be a lie. You better make your answer to Kennery a lie, Con."

"You make up the lie, then," Con countered.

Seeley started to speak and then didn't, but his face remained set in stubborn disapproval.

When Seeley didn't speak, Brayton went on, "What's the harm in the truth? He already knows we're up for trial, he already knows we want Joe dead, and he's willing to kill him for us. If he hasn't already guessed that Joe is tied in with Schaeffer's killing, he's pretty dumb."

"All right," Seeley said. "Tell'm, but hold out the one thing, Con." He paused and asked with seeming irrelevance, "Con, you think I'd stop at killing you if you put my neck in a noose?"

Brayton stood for a moment and then said truthfully, "No, you'd kill me."

"You better believe I will. Now here's what you tell Kennery. You tell him why you and Dad had Schaeffer killed. You tell him why Joe Potatoes has to be put away. But just remember, never bring in my name. Schaeffer's killing — Joe done it alone. You got that, Con? Joe done it alone."

"You don't care, then, if we tell him the true story?"

"Not one damn bit. Just so I'm left out of it. Do it that way, Con, and I'm happy. Don't do it and you're dead."

Brayton nodded. "What a helluva commotion over something so simple." He moved away from the wall, pushed past Seeley, and went in the room. Seeley trailed him in.

Sam had heard their low conversation through the door, but not the exact words of it, and he sipped thoughtfully at his drink. He was aware of Herrington watching him with an expression of quiet approval in his heavy face. He kept his own face expressionless, but he was reviewing what had just passed. Had he pushed them too far, too soon? No, he didn't think he had. Any prudent killer would first assess the consequences before killing a man, and that was exactly what he was doing.

Presently the murmuring in the hall ceased, and Brayton returned, followed by Seeley, and approached Herrington. "Dad, Seeley's agreed. Let me talk, will you?"

When Herrington nodded, Brayton returned to the bed. "Here's the way it is, Sam. There was a key witness for the government on his way to testify against us in our trial. He was a lying, double-crossing crook that worked for me at the agency, and I should have fired him years ago. We couldn't let him testify. We paid this Indian — Joe Potatoes, we called him — to get Schaeffer, and he did. Maybe you read about it or heard about it?"

"No."

"Well, like a lot of Indians, Joe loves his booze. He's blackmailing us now, and there'll be no end to it. After he's dead, nothing will happen. You got to take my word for that, Sam. If he was a chief or a member of the tribal council, that would be different, but Joe's a nothing. Nobody likes him and nobody trusts him. If they find him dead of pneumonia, nobody'll be surprised. If they find him shot, they'll figure somebody got even with him, and believe me, a lot of people had reason to. His wife is a whore and her family's disowned her." He paused. "That satisfy you, Sam?"

For answer, Sam looked at Seeley. "That's pretty small stuff, Seeley."

Carnes actually blushed. "Now I hear it spoke, I reckon it is."

Sam turned to Brayton. "Half down now, and half

when I get him — that all right?"

Both men reached for their wallets at the same time. Both men were smiling. Between them, they rounded up enough eagles to make Sam's hundred, then had another drink in celebration.

Afterwards, Brayton took over the chore of instructing Sam. He got only as far as telling him to take tomorrow afternoon's train north as far as the stop called Boundary, when Seeley interrupted. "Con, why don't you take Sam down to the bar and finish that? Me and Dad got some Texas talk to chew over. We'll be down when we're through."

Brayton looked surprised, and his glance shuttled to Herrington. Herrington looked surprised too, but he only nodded.

Brayton rose. "Come along, Sam."

When they had left the room, closing the door behind them, Herrington, still in his chair, said curiously, "What Texas talk, Seeley?"

Carnes moved over to the bed, where he could face his boss, and sat down. He began, quietly, "Dad, we're makin' a mistake hirin' Kennery."

"Prove it."

"I can't. It's just a feelin' I've got."

Herrington scowled, and his glance at Seeley was at once searching and skeptical. "Funny. The feeling I've got is that we've found the right man. What's there about him that spooks you?"

"Nothin' spooks me. Nothin' ever spooks me," Carnes said flatly.

"The hell it don't," Herrington replied roughly. "I noticed, when Con came back from talking with you out in the hall, he never told Kennery you were with Joe."

"Damn right he didn't. I told him he'd better not tie me in."

"So you're not spooked," Herrington said dryly.

Carnes came to his feet, and Herrington saw that he had scored. Seeley was white around the mouth, and his bleached eyes held a wicked glint. "Careful, Dad."

"All right, all right," Herrington said placatingly. "I'm just trying to understand you. Here we got this whole thing set up and paid for, and now you're backin' off. Why?"

"I'm not backin' off," Carnes said sullenly. "I'm only tryin' to warn you."

"Damn it, Seeley, be reasonable!" Herrington exploded. "What else could we do? There ain't time to send for someone we know. And you can't stand out in front of the hotel and say to everybody that comes along. 'Want two hundred dollars for killin' an Indian?' Me, I think we're blind lucky."

"What if he takes the money and runs?"

"That's a risk," Herrington conceded. "One we got to take, too."

"What if he goes to the law?" Carnes persisted.

"Why, if he does, we call him a liar. There's the word of the three of us that we made him no such a proposition."

"Aah," Seeley said in disgust. Turning, he put his hand under the back of his belt and began to slowly circle the open space of the room.

Herrington leaned forward now, elbows on knees, forearms crossed. "This ain't like you, Seeley. Name me one thing about him that looks wrong."

Seeley halted and looked at his boss. "All right. Where's this friend he's been expectin'? If he's so damn set on meetin' him, why would he take four or five days off to earn two hundred dollars?"

Big Dad snorted. "Why, his friend's kept Sam waitin'. Why shouldn't Sam keep his friend waitin'?"

"If there *is* a friend," Carnes said cynically.

"We can't know that, and why does it matter a damn if there's no friend? If Kennery runs out on us, we've lost one hundred dollars. If he delivers, we're safe. He can't talk, and we won't talk. Can you shoot that down, Seeley?"

Carnes resumed his pacing, shaking his head from side to side many times. "It's just a feelin' I got, Dad. This is no good."

Big Dad rose to his feet. "Well, you're out of it and safe, Seeley. It's me and Con that takes the risk, not you."

"Well, I'm goin' to watch him," Carnes said flatly.

"Go ahead, but you got damn good eyes if you can see as far as that Indian reservation."

His donkey's laugh followed this, and Carnes looked at him with malevolence in his pale eyes.

"Let's go drink up, Seeley," Herrington said. "They'll be wondering what's keeping us."

He moved past Carnes toward the door. Then, as if something had just occurred to him, he halted and turned. "Don't pick a fight with him, Seeley," Dad said quietly. "Let him get this job done. Afterwards, I don't care." He paused and then smiled. "Yes, I do care. I like you, Seeley. I'd hate to have to bury you."

Six

Around midnight, Sam parted from Brayton, Herrington, and Carnes in the second-floor corridor. Their good nights were alcoholically cordial, and Sam went the short distance to his own room and let himself in. After lighting the lamp on the dresser, he moved over to the bed, propped up the pillow, and leaned back against it, half-reclining. From his jacket pocket he took the letter of introduction that Con Brayton had given him. It was addressed to Roy McCook, who, Brayton said, was a friend who ran the trading post at Boundary, and who would supply him with whiskey and a horse. The envelope was unsealed, and Sam read it. It was simply a request to McCook to supply Sam with everything he asked for.

He tossed the letter on the bed and reviewed this incredible day. He had been hired almost casually to kill the Indian who had killed Schaeffer. It was an unbelievable piece of luck for him, but when he analyzed it, he was not much farther along toward getting evidence on Carnes than he had been this morning. True, he had the name of the Indian implicated in Schaeffer's killing, and he had evidence, unprovable in court, that Herrington and Brayton had paid him to kill the Indian. What, he wondered, had Carnes said to Brayton out in the hall this afternoon, and what had Carnes said to Herrington under the guise of "Texas talk"? So far, neither by words nor by any actions of the three, did he have anything to tie in Carnes with Schaeffer's killing. There was only Carnes' shotgun and his date of arrival in Primrose. In sum, nothing.

Sheriff Morehead, Sam knew, should be told of what had happened today, and of his pending visit to the reservation. He realized then that he did not know where Morehead lived, and even if he did, he couldn't talk to him without risking being seen, even tomorrow morning. It would be insanely risky to go to the courthouse to see the sheriff. If he saw him in the street or at the depot, the risk of being seen talking with him was still there. Yet Morehead should know what had passed and what was coming up.

It came to him then that there was a way to communicate with Morehead without having to speak with him. Rising now, Sam moved over to the lamp, blew it out, then crossed to the door, fumbled for the knob, found it, and opened the door. The second floor was quiet. The only sounds he could hear were the distant, muted talk and laughter that came up the stairwell from the barroom. Stepping out in the hall, he quietly closed the door behind him and then slowly moved down to Brayton's room. Here he halted and listened, and presently he picked up the sound of deep, rhythmical breathing.

Moving on now to the room next door, which held Herrington and Carnes, he halted again. The sound of raucous snoring reached him through the door. He tried and failed to pick up the sound of a second person's breathing, which the snoring drowned out. It didn't matter really, for the snoring would cover any small sound he might make on his way to the stairwell.

He went down the steps, crossed the dimly lit lobby, and descended the veranda steps to the plank walk. Turning right, he moved on past the veranda and the street entrance to the saloon, and turned right at the corner. Passing the blank back of the saloon, he made out the bay of the loading dock for the kitchen. The small one-story wing off the kitchen would be Tenney's and her mother's room. He halted now, letting his eyes adjust to the darkness, and presently he made out the shape of a rain barrel at the corner of the wing, and then the door that was the outside entrance to their room. Approaching it now, he knocked firmly on the door, then put his back against the wall next to it. The door opened, casting a shaft of lamplight on the ground.

"Who is it?" Tenney asked.

"It's me — Sam. Douse the lamp, Tenney, and let me in."

He waited until the lamp was blown out, and then stepped into a room whose furnishings he could not even see. Halting a step inside the door, he felt Tenney brushing his sleeve as she closed the door.

"What is it, Sam?" Tenney whispered. Before he could answer, Mrs. Payne's voice came from the doorway of the other room.

"I'm awake, Tenney."

"I'm sorry I had to do this, Mrs. Payne, but it's the only way I can talk with you."

"That's all right," Mrs. Payne said.

Unable to see either woman, Sam felt their friendly presence. "Tenney, can you see Sheriff Morehead tomorrow morning and give him a message?"

"Of course I can," Tenney answered from behind him.

"Tell him I'm heading for the reservation tomorrow. I don't know how long I'll be gone. Tell him I was paid tonight by Herrington and Brayton to kill the Indian they say shot Schaeffer."

"They paid you?" Tenney asked incredulously.

"A hundred dollars now. A hundred dollars when he's dead."

Mrs. Payne's voice came from a new and closer position.

"Can't they be arrested for that?"

"Yes, but not yet. Tell Morehead to stay away from them. Also, if he plans to see the train off tomorrow, tell him not to. Tell him if he sees me on the street before train time, not to stop me or talk with me. You might tell him, too, that if I knew where he lived I wouldn't have bothered you tonight."

"Important things aren't bothers," Mrs. Payne said quietly.

"One more thing, Mrs. Payne. I told you to keep my badge until I called for it. I'd like it now." He heard the rustle of her nightdress as she left the room.

"Sam, if you don't kill this man, won't they know and turn on you?" Tenney seemed very close to him when she spoke: he even caught a pleasant smell of newly washed, sun-dried hair.

"I wish they'd try, Tenney. It would make things a lot easier, but not to your question. I think I'll have the goods on Carnes before they know we have the Indian." He felt a touch on his arm, and then Mrs.

Payne said. "Here's the badge, Sam."

Sam thanked her and said, "I don't know when I'll see you two again, but I will. Goodbye for now."

They wished him good night, and Sam stepped out into the darkness. The night was so quiet that he could hear the distant thudding of the Consolidated Stamping Mill, working its night shift across the river. From up street at the livery, he could hear the quiet nickering of a couple of horses back in the corral.

He was almost past the loading dock when he caught the faint scent of burnt tobacco. It took him the space of the two steps that put him past the loading dock before his memory was jogged. This was the smell of Seeley Carnes' raw Mexican tobacco, with which he had become so familiar these last few days.

He didn't break stride as he headed for the corner. If that smoke had come from Seeley Carnes' cigarette, it meant that Carnes had perhaps seen him go into Tenney's place, and had certainly seen him come out. Quiet dismay touched him for a moment. Was Carnes following him? If he was, it meant his actions were suspect to Brayton and Herrington.

Rounding the corner, Sam flattened himself against the front of the saloon. How would they interpret his visit to Tenney? A tryst? Hardly, with Mrs. Payne there.

Sam poked his head around the corner and looked down the dark alley. He thought he saw something moving in the darkness, but he couldn't be sure. Deciding to take the chance, he moved back around the corner, flattening himself against the saloon wall. He had taken less than a dozen cautious steps when he heard pounding on a door down the alley. Swiftly, and as quietly as he could, he moved along the wall toward the loading dock. He had barely reached its bay when a shaft of lamplight appeared from Tenney's door. It revealed Carnes standing in the alley, facing the door.

Sam heard Carnes say, "Miss, I was coming down the alley and I saw a man go in your place."

Tenney's voice came to him faintly as she said, "Surely you're mistaken."

"No. I'm not. Look around in there."

"But the door was locked," Tenney said.

Carnes said flatly, "I seen what I seen. Look around in there. I'll help you." Carnes stepped up to the door.

By the diminution of the lamplight, Sam knew that Tenney was trying to shut the door on Carnes, but suddenly the lamplight increased and Carnes disappeared inside.

Sam ran then, heading for the door. Even as he ran, the lamplight faded. Did it mean that Tenney had fled to her mother's room? He could hear nothing except the pounding of his own feet as he reached the door and lunged through it. Tenney was standing in a back corner of the tiny living room, holding her wrapper across her nightgown with one hand, and holding the lamp with the other. When she turned her head to the doorway, Sam could see the fright in her face. He hauled up just as Seeley Carnes stepped out of the bedroom.

At sight of Sam, he halted and the two men looked at each other.

"What are you doing in this house?" Sam asked.

"I saw a man come in here and they won't believe

it. But he's hid there."

Sam moved toward him. "If you saw him come in here, you saw him go out. It was me."

"Then what were you doin' here?" Carnes demanded.

Behind Carnes, Sam could see the dim figure of Mrs. Payne standing back in the room.

"Not that it's any of your damn business, Seeley, but I came to tell Tenney and her mother goodbye."

"You could have told them in the morning," Carnes said coldly.

Now Sam moved toward him. He saw the fingers of Seeley's right hand unclench, and he saw beyond it the form of Mrs. Payne, moving out of the way into the darkness.

"Again, it's none of your business, Seeley, but I'll be long gone by daylight."

"You're goin' to Junction City on the train," Seeley said flatly.

"And I'll catch it ten miles out of town at the Calico Flats switch-off."

"Why?"

Sam replied contemptuously, "So a certain Mr. Morehead won't telegraph ahead and have me watched." He added then, with quiet menace in his voice, "You have a long nose, Seeley. I aim to change the shape of it."

Carnes' hand streaked for his gun, and he had just grasped the butt of it as Sam finished his lunge. Sam's left hand clamped down on the wrist of Carnes' gun-hand, sealing the pistol in its holster. At the same time, with his right arm bent, Sam rammed his elbow in

Carnes' face with a savage, full-bodied swing.

Carnes stumbled back against the doorframe, instinctively raising his left hand to his face. Sam felt Carnes' right hand tug, and now he lifted Seeley's wrist. The gun came out of the holster and was barely clear of it when Sam swept down his right hand and batted the revolver out of Carnes' hand. It clattered to the floor at Tenney's feet.

Carnes, with his back against the doorframe now, had a position that could anchor his weight. He braced his foot against the wall, lowered his head, and drove at Sam, trying to butt him with his head. It caught Sam on the shoulder and spun him around off-balance, but he still held Carnes' wrist with his left hand and, falling, he pulled Carnes two steps forward, and then, using his falling weight as a lever, Sam yanked on Carnes' arm. The Texan was propelled past him in a staggering, off-balance lunge. Sam's back hit the floor with a crash that drove the breath from him in an anguished grunt. He rolled over in time to see Carnes, far off-balance and running, trip on the doorsill and sprawl face down in the alley. He had regained his knees when Sam came hurtling through the doorway and smashed him flat in the alley's dust.

Moaning softly, Tenney came up to the doorway, still holding the lamp. She arrived in time to see both men, hatless now, come to their feet facing each other, and she noticed that Seeley Carnes was bleeding from the torn lip that Sam's elbow had mashed. Now the real fight began, with the whole alley to maneuver in. On the first move, Sam was the quicker. He came at Carnes, accepting a clout on the side of his head as the price of closing in. He drove a solid, ramming blow into Carnes' midriff, and Tenney could hear the great explosion of Carnes' breath that followed. Carnes instinctively wrapped his arms around his middle and bent over. Sam moved a half-step to his right, then drove his fist into the side of Carnes' face. The force of the blow spun Carnes half around and off-balance, so that he stumbled across the alley, head down, and rammed headfirst into the door of the sturdy shed that stored the hotel hack at night. Sam caught him on the rebound, putting both hands on Carnes' shoulders and yanking him around. Carnes spun and, coming out of the spin, kicked out with his right leg. The blow caught Sam behind the knee, pulling that leg out from under him so that he pitched on his side. Rolling over to come to his knees, he caught another kick that knifed into his side. Rising now, he heard the great, shuddering inhalations as Carnes fought to get his breath back. Sam tested his numb left leg, found that it would hold him, and moved in again, this time with a determined fury that frightened Tenney and her mother, who were watching from the door. Carnes fought viciously, trying to stop Sam's slugging advance, to reverse their roles, to take the fight to Sam, instead of being relentlessly pushed back. He was fighting equally hard to regain his breath.

With a kind of dogged, killer stubbornness, Sam moved Carnes back. The blows that Sam couldn't check or parry, he accepted silently, always moving forward, always punishing Carnes' body, never his head.

Slowly, Carnes was backed toward the corner of the

house, where a great rain barrel sat in the loading dock's bay.

Carnes backed around the house and into the barrel, and sought to step around it, but Sam, his quarry cornered now, had no intention of letting him escape. This was where the fight would finish. He drove Carnes back between the barrel and the wall, then slugged blow after blow into the Texan's lean body. Again, Carnes made the mistake of lowering his arms to protect his midriff. Instantly, Sam went for Carnes' head. He drove a jab into the Texan's jaw that smashed his head back against the building's clapboard. Finally, with a blow that caught Carnes' rebounding head on the tip of the jaw, the fight ended. Carnes' knees buckled and he fell face-forward into Sam's arms. With one hand on Carnes' chest, Sam pushed him back against the wall, and then, holding Carnes erect, he reached down into the big barrel. It was half-full.

Then he knelt, took his hand away from Carnes' chest, and let his body slack over his shoulder. Lifting him then, Sam dropped him, jackknifed, into the rain barrel. The water geysered up, and when it had settled, Sam saw that its level was just under Carnes' chin. The Texan's legs, rendered unable to bend at the knees by the confining barrel, pointed straight into the air.

Sam stumbled around the barrel, reached the loading dock, folded his arms on it, and put his head on his arms. Only then was he aware that Tenney and her mother had come out into the alley with the lamp to watch the fight's finish. He heard Tenney and her mother come up behind him now, but for the moment he could only fight for more and more air to breathe.

When his wild panting lessened, he straightened up, wincing at the pain the smallest movement caused him. Turning his head now, he saw Tenney, lamp in hand, and her mother, standing close beside him.

Mrs. Payne held his hat out to him and then said quietly, "He'll never get out of that barrel without help, Sam."

"You feel like helpin' him, Mrs. Payne?" Sam asked dryly.

"No, but if I call myself a Christian, I ought to."

Sam nodded and tramped slowly back to the barrel. Once there, he put both hands on its rim and pulled the barrel toward him. It tipped on its side with a thud and a cascade of water, which swirled around Carnes' body. Grabbing Carnes by the collar of his jacket, Sam dragged him out of the barrel and let him fall on his back in the mud.

Now he looked at Mrs. Payne and said, "That's a comfortable place to rest, Mrs. Payne. I've used it a couple of times myself."

Mrs. Payne smiled. "All right, let's leave him there."

"Are you hurt, Sam?" Tenney asked.

"All over," Sam said. "I can make it to bed though." He looked at Tenney's mother and said, "Mrs. Payne, he may be at you again. Stick to my story. I came to you yesterday afternoon while Herrington and Brayton were with their lawyer. I asked your permission to see Tenney. You didn't like me much, but left it up to Tenney. I was going to take her to the church social tomorrow night. The reason I came to your house was to tell Tenney I'd be out of town for a few days. I didn't tell you where I was going, or how. That's absolutely all you know."

"I'll remember," Mrs. Payne said. She looked down at Carnes. "Why did he come to our place?"

"He doesn't trust me, Mrs. Payne. He followed me here and waited until I left. I think he thought I was meeting Sheriff Morehead in your rooms, and that he'd find Morehead there if he searched the place." Now Sam looked at Tenney. "Tenney, tell Morehead about this too. You can forget about warning him to stay away from me. I've got to leave before daylight to back up my story to Carnes."

"What will Brayton and Herrington do about your beating up their friend?"

"Laugh, I reckon," Sam said. "I'll say good night now."

Seven

Tenney, wearing a coat over her uniform against the morning chill, was at the courthouse by seven-thirty the next morning. As she turned down the corridor, she saw Sheriff Morehead unlocking the door of his office at the rear corner of the building. She was congratulating herself on her timing when Morehead turned and started for the side door. He wasn't unlocking his office, but locking it, Tenney saw, and she called, "Oh, Sheriff!"

Morehead turned, and Tenney hurried to meet him. As she halted before him, Morehead said in his gravel voice, "Why, hello, Tenney."

"Can I talk with you, please?"

"Can you make it later on, Tenney? I was headed for the depot."

"That can wait. You've got to hear what I have to tell you."

Morehead looked at her strangely and then moved past her, reaching in his pocket for his key. Unlocking the door, he stood aside and Tenney moved into his office. Morehead gestured to the chair beside the desk, where Tenney seated herself, then he took off his hat and seated himself in his own swivel chair, behind the desk. "What is it, Tenney?" Morehead asked.

"It's about Sam Kennery," Tenney said, and she

told him about Kennery's midnight visit.

As she talked, bewilderment and incredulity came into Morehead's square face.

Tenney stopped speaking, halted by his expression, and then said, "What did I say?"

"You mean you know Kennery's a deputy U.S. marshal?"

Suddenly Tenney realized that events had moved so rapidly for Sam Kennery that he had not even had time to see the sheriff.

She began at the beginning then, telling him how she had surprised Kennery picking the lock of Herrington's room, then of his visit to the kitchen, of his identifying himself and asking her and her mother for help. She told of watching Sam's search of Herrington's and Carnes' room, and of his finding a shotgun in Carnes' blanket roll. As she progressed to the events of the late evening, when Kennery was offered and had accepted money for killing the Indian who was implicated in Schaeffer's murder, Morehead could only look at her with undisguised amazement and embarrassment. When she paused for breath, Morehead shook his head.

He said wryly, "I feel like a man with an unfaithful wife. He's always the last to know. I'm the sheriff here, and you're the one who tells me what my marshal friend has been doing."

"I haven't told all of it yet, Sheriff." She told him then of Seeley Carnes' visit after Sam had left, and of Sam's return and the subsequent fight.

Morehead listened to it with pure pleasure. When she finished, the sheriff said, "Won't that beating change Herrington's and Brayton's mind about Sam?"

"I don't think it did." Tenney answered. "The reason I don't is that first thing this morning I went up to Sam's room. It was empty and his blanket roll was gone. If they called it off last night, Sam wouldn't have gone, would he?"

"Certainly he would," Morehead said. "Fired or not, he'd be off to get that Indian, wouldn't he?"

"But he'd have taken the train instead of pretending he didn't want you to see him."

Morehead nodded. "That's true. Now go back, Tenney. Does Kennery think Carnes was with the Indian when Schaeffer was shot?"

"I think he does. I think he hopes the Indian will give him proof." She leaned forward in her chair and asked, "Who is Kennery, Sheriff? I know he's a deputy U.S. marshal, but who is he?"

"That's what I asked in my letter to Marshal Wilbarth. He quoted me a letter from Kennery's boss. Kennery was a rancher up north. He was going to marry a girl. It seems she was a teacher in a tough cattle town that was at the center of a range war. She got caught in the crossfire of cowboys shooting it out on the street."

Tenney asked the inevitable question: "Was she killed?"

Morehead dipped his head affirmatively. "The sheriff there was a coward and afraid to take sides. Kennery went to the U.S. marshal and asked to be deputized so he'd have the law behind him when he hunted down her killers. He did just that. Afterwards, he wanted to resign and did, but his marshal kept reappointing him and assigning him jobs. Kennery finally gave in because, as he put it to his chief, he was making a career out of mourning for the dead girl." Morehead spread his hands and shrugged. "That's about all I know of him, Tenney, except that his chief said he was far and away the best man ever to wear the badge in his district."

Tenney was silent for a moment. "How sad," she said quietly.

Sheriff Morehead said gently, "Any sadder than your mother losing a young husband? Any sadder than you not even remembering your father?"

Tenney stood up. "I guess not, but nobody should feel sorry for me. You don't miss what you can't remember."

Morehead rose too, now. "Well, Tenney, you've earned a deputy's badge over these last few days. Still, I don't think a person should wear one who's never shaved, do you?"

Tenney laughed, and Morehead gave her his small smile. "Keep in touch with me, Tenney. That's the only way I'll know what's going on around here."

Eight

Sam caught the Primrose & Northern at the Calico Flats spur, where the train halted to pick up a couple of cattle cars. He turned his horse loose to find its way back to town, and boarded the car with his saddle and blanket roll. He had the whole afternoon to speculate on how Herrington and Brayton would react to his beating of Seeley Carnes.

His exhausted sleep of last night, after the fight, had been uninterrupted. If they had been angry with him, or if they had changed their minds about hiring him to kill Joe Potatoes, they would have awakened him and told him the deal was off. Since they hadn't, he assumed that they still wanted him to go through with the murder. A corollary was that they had believed what Carnes undoubtedly told them of events leading to the fight. Carnes would have had to tell them that he broke into the house of Kennery's girl and got beat up for his pains. As far as Sam could see, nothing was changed. But no, there was one single change, an unimportant one: Seeley Carnes' dislike of him was changed into genuine hatred now.

The train from the south arrived at Junction City after dark, just as the one from the north did, but later. As he had done before, Sam gave his bedroll and saddle to the driver of the Prairie House hack, and made his way again by back streets to the capitol building. Sam had no doubt that the dogs that had barked at him before were the same ones that barked at him tonight. The State House held fewer lighted windows than on his previous visit, and Sam wondered, tramping the bricks up to the marble steps, if Marshal Wilbarth and Newford had already called it a day.

The marble corridors of the building held a few lighted lamps; the basement corridor was lighted too, and the same pencil of light showed under the door of the marshal's office.

Sam knocked and entered and saw Marshal Wilbarth in shirtsleeves, seated at his rolltop desk at the rear of the room on the left. Wilbarth rose at his entrance, picked up the lamp, and came toward him. Holding the lamp in his left hand, Wilbarth unsmilingly extended his hand, saying, "Back so soon, Kennery?"

"You can thank Sheriff Morehead for that," Sam said.

Wilbarth put the lamp on the big table and gestured to the chair opposite him, and Sam sank into it and took off his hat. As Wilbarth seated himself, Sam noted the dark circles under his eyes. His face was astonishingly pale; Sam wondered if the man had been in the sunshine an hour in the past two weeks.

Wilbarth observed dryly, "You've been in a fight."

Sam started to raise his hand to his bruised cheekbone, then let it drop. "That's right."

"Well, what have you got for me?" Wilbarth asked him patiently.

Sam reviewed the faked saloon quarrel with Morehead that led to his introduction to and acceptance by Herrington, Brayton, and Carnes, and he told of his efforts to establish himself as a thoroughly undesirable character.

"The real break came," Sam said, "when I was caught picking the lock of Herrington's room by Tenney Payne. I talked her into taking me down to the kitchen to meet her mother before turning me in to the owner of the hotel. I told the two of them I was a deputy U.S. marshal, and something about the case I'm working on."

"You told the girl and her mother that?" Wilbarth asked incredulously.

"How else could I explain the lock-picking and the room search? How else could I find out from the hotel register when Seeley Carnes had arrived at Primrose?"

"Then you're known all over Primrose by now."

"Is that a fact or a guess?" Sam asked dryly.

"Well, a guess, but a good one, I think," Wilbarth said grimly. "A woman will keep a secret about herself, but damned if she'll keep anybody else's secret." He sighed. "Well, go on."

Sam told Wilbarth how he had found the shotgun in Carnes' room and established his date of arrival, which was two days after Schaeffer had been ambushed.

"You think there's any connection?"

"Tell me your guess when I've finished," Sam said. Then he told of the meeting last night in Herrington's room, when he had been hired to do the murder. As the story progressed, Wilbarth's face suddenly came alive and he leaned forward, his gray eyes bright with excitement. When Sam reached in his pocket and put on the table the hundred dollars in gold eagles he had received as an advance payment for killing Joe Potatoes, Wilbarth stared at them with incredulity. Sam went on then to tell of the curious reluctance of Seeley Carnes to have Brayton reveal the reason for their wanting the Indian killed. Sam finished by saying, "What did Con Brayton say to Carnes out in the hall that made him change his mind?"

Wilbarth thought a moment. "Likely promised to keep him out of it, wouldn't you judge?"

"So you think there were two men assigned to kill Schaeffer?"

"Why, that's obvious," Wilbarth said irritably.

"It's so obvious that you didn't bother to tell me you suspected there were two men. I had to go through the files of the *Capital Times* to have Red Macandy point it out in print."

Wilbarth looked at him unbelievingly. "My God, you mean neither of us told you?" He watched Sam shake his head, and raised his hand to his closed eyes with his thumb and index finger. "I *am* sorry, Kennery. Anse and I have been short on sleep for too long." He let his hand drop now. "Yes, there had to be two men, and after what you've told me, I think Carnes is the other. And to answer your question, I think Brayton promised to keep Carnes out of it and let Joe Potatoes take the whole blame."

"Joe Potatoes," Sam mused. "What kind of name is that, Marshal?"

"The name Brayton gave him, I reckon," Wilbarth said contemptuously. "Brayton won't learn their language, and he can't remember or pronounce their names, so he names them himself. They learn to answer to it and that's all he cares about."

Wilbarth rose and moved over to his desk. From one of its drawers he drew forth an envelope. Returning to the table, he picked up the eagles and put them in the envelope and sealed it. Then he sat down and said, "Now, about the fight?"

Sam told him of last night's events that had led up to his brawl with Carnes. He added his own opinion that since neither Brayton nor Herrington had demanded an accounting from him, the situation was unchanged.

Wilbarth nodded in agreement. "You've done a fine job so far, Kennery."

"Thanks, but it's a girl who did more of it."

"Well, a girl can't do the rest of it," the marshal said. "Tomorrow you take the train north. Anse will be on the same train, but you won't be traveling together and you won't talk to each other. Do just what Brayton told you to do. Look up McCook and give him Brayton's letter. By the way, is it sealed?"

Sam shook his head, reached in the pocket of his duck jacket, brought out the letter, and tossed it in front of Wilbarth. "Just the usual. Marshal. 'This is a friend of mine, give him what he asks for' type of letter."

Wilbarth read the scribbled note, returned it to its envelope, and without comment, tossed it to Sam. "Anse will take the stage from Boundary to the agency. I'll give him some harmless job that will keep him hanging around the agency post. I doubt if this Joe Potatoes will recognize him, but it doesn't matter if he does. He'll keep you in sight at all times. Try to pick up Joe at night. Take him down to the stock pens south of the agency before you give him Brayton's message. What was that message?"

"That I'm carrying money and whiskey for him from Brayton."

The marshal nodded. "Anse will see you pick up Joe, and he'll be down at the pens waiting for you. After you've taken Joe, you'll both head for Crater. That's the county seat of Summit County, and it's a two-day ride from the agency. I'll be waiting for you at the county courthouse there. Anse will have the warrant."

"Suspicion of murder?"

Wilbarth nodded. "The sheriff up there is an old friend of mine. I was his deputy once. I'll tell him the public story if anyone is interested — that Joe has been smuggling whiskey into the reservation. You'll have the evidence with you."

"You think Joe will talk right away, Marshal?"

"I doubt it. You said Brayton told you Joe understood English?"

At Sam's nod, the marshal said grimly, "Well, we'll let him overhear enough to scare hell out of him."

"Will I stay with you there for the questioning?"

"Not long. You'll have taken time enough as it is. If Joe talks enough later to implicate Carnes, I'll get word to you through Morehead."

The marshal yawned, and Sam, taking the hint, rose

108

and was reaching for his hat when a sharp, almost insolent knock came at the door.

Sam looked at Wilbarth, who jabbed a finger toward a door in the side wall behind Sam. Sam grabbed his hat and moved swiftly to the door, opened it, stepped inside a small storeroom, and closed the door. The knock came again, and Sam heard Wilbarth call irritably, "Who is it? Come in." He heard the corridor door open, and then Wilbarth said sourly, "Oh, hello, Red."

"Who were you talking to, Marshal?" a surly voice asked.

"If I was talking, I was talking in my sleep," the marshal said. "What are you doing here, Red?"

"Covering a late committee meeting upstairs. The *Times* never sleeps, you know. I was headed home when I saw the light in your office, so I came back. You got anything for me, Marshal?"

"Nothing but contempt. For you *and* your damned newspaper," Wilbarth said calmly.

This, then, was Red Macandy, the *Capital Times* editor, Sam thought. He was surprised at Wilbarth's open rudeness.

"Come, come, Marshal, it's men like me that make you boys at the trough earn your swill." His voice was taunting, and Sam leaned down and peered through the keyhole. Wilbarth was out of his line of vision, but Red Macandy was squarely in it. He was a dumpy, jowly, middle-aged man, dressed in a rumpled townsman's suit. A half-chewed, unlit cigar was wedged in the corner of his mouth. As Sam watched, Macandy removed the cigar, which, exposed now, was simply a great wet wad of chewed tobacco. He pointed it at Wilbarth. "The government got another week's postponement on the Brayton trial yesterday. What are you —" he stabbed the cigar again at Wilbarth — "you, yourself, doing to earn that postponement?"

Wilbarth's usually mild voice hardened as he spoke. "You want me to name witnesses so they can be shot too?"

"Come on. I know your witnesses. That's public information."

Through the keyhole, Sam saw the light diminish and guessed that Wilbarth had removed the lamp from the table to his desk.

"Go home, Red," Wilbarth said wearily.

He saw Red Macandy look at the door of the storeroom, then he moved swiftly out of Sam's vision. When he appeared again, he was on the near side of the table and close. Rising, Sam clamped his hand on the doorknob. Only seconds later he felt the doorknob strain against his grip. He held the knob immovable, and then he heard Wilbarth's sharp command: "Get away from there, Red."

"There's somebody inside holding that knob!" Red snarled.

"Then you better give up and get out," Wilbarth said stonily. "I'm locking up."

"But there's somebody in there," Red insisted.

"If there is, she can spend the night there," Wilbarth said. "There's a cot inside, a dusty one, but still a cot."

"She?" Red asked.

Wilbarth said wearily, "You snooping fool. That lock has been jammed for a month. Why do you think

I've got all that junk on the top of my desk? Anse's desk too? Get out. Red. I'm blowing the light."

"Very funny," Red said sourly, and Sam heard him move away. He heard Wilbarth's footfalls as he moved the length of the room, then the metallic sound of a door being locked. Cautiously, he opened the storeroom door and moved into the lightless room. In the darkness, he tiptoed to the corridor door and tried it. Sure enough, Wilbarth had locked him in. Sam went back to the storeroom, took out a match, and scraped it alight on his bootsole. There was the cot with blankets on it that Wilbarth had mentioned. As the match died, Sam smiled. Like him or not, Wilbarth was a tough one, Sam thought. It didn't matter that Red Macandy probably didn't believe Wilbarth's story about the jammed door, and did believe that someone was in the storeroom. What did matter was that Red didn't know who it was.

Sam was undressing when he heard the corridor door being rattled. He moved quietly across the room, guessing that Red Macandy had returned on the off-chance that Wilbarth had come back to free whoever was in the closet. There was a long silence, and then he heard Red Macandy's growling curse: "Bastards!"

Long before daylight, Wilbarth let himself into his office and Sam awoke. "Get any sleep, Kennery?" The marshal spoke from the doorway into the total darkness.

"All I want."

"Better move out now, while it's dark. Red might

be here early. For all I know, he may have somebody watching outside now, so don't strike a light."

As Sam pulled on his boots and felt around for his jacket, he told Wilbarth of Red's return after the marshal had left. They both laughed, and afterwards, Wilbarth said soberly, "That was a close one, Kennery, and could have meant real trouble. If he'd seen you, he'd have asked around and found someone who saw you on the Primrose train. He'd have checked in Primrose, tied you in with Herrington and Carnes, and then he'd have dragged me into it. He probably would have accused me of making a deal with that pair, with you as the go-between. Whatever he wrote, though, would have tipped off our three blackbirds."

Sam felt for his jacket in the dark. "I sent my saddle and blanket roll to the Prairie House in the hack. How do I get them without showing myself?"

"Anything in your blanket roll that would identify you?"

Sam thought for a moment and said, "No."

"Then leave them. McCook will outfit you."

They moved out into the dimly lit corridor, but instead of ascending the stairs to the lobby above, Wilbarth continued down the hall and they exited through an outside basement stairway. They parted at its head, but not before Wilbarth said, "See you in Crater, Kennery. Good luck."

Nine

The *Capital Times* office, a block off Main Street, was wedged between a saddle-and-harness shop and a hardware store; it was a narrow building whose wide front window was painted white up half of its height. This morning, both the printer and Billy Foster, Red's reporter and ad salesman, were there ahead of him. Red gave them a surly good morning, peeled off his coat, and took out from his side pocket the notes of last night's committee meeting, then sat down at the square desk placed midway between the window and the railing that separated the pressroom from the office.

Before Red seated himself, he said to Billy Foster, a handsome, curly-haired young man dressed in a suit that would have graced a whiskey drummer, "Get out of here, Billy. Get us some money."

"You want me to hit Governor Halsey's office this morning?"

"No, the marshal's. Ask him who he was hiding from me last night."

Billy rose and headed for the coatrack. "Will he tell me?"

"Of course not. Ask him anyway. Get him mad."

Billy got his hat and left, and Red sat down and began to scribble out his story of the senate finance committee meeting last night.

When he was finished with the story, he went back and gave it to his printer, and then returned to his desk. Taking a cigar from one of the desk drawers, he fired it up and then tilted back in his swivel chair. He had a game that he often played in idle moments, which consisted of trying to identify his fellow townsmen by their headgear, the only part of them visible above the opaque lower half of the window. This morning, however, the game had lost its savor. He was thinking without any charity of his meeting last night with Marshal Wilbarth. He was positive he'd heard Wilbarth talking to someone when he knocked on the door, and that whoever it was had hidden in the closet and held the knob to prevent the door from being opened.

Who was it? And why the secrecy?

Reasoning closely now, Red was certain that Wilbarth knew he was in deep trouble on two counts, the first of which was that the marshal's office had allowed a key witness in the Brayton-Herrington fraud case to be murdered in the presence of a deputy marshal, thus destroying the government's case. The other count was that Wilbarth, his regular deputy, and his special deputies had failed to unearth even a clue as to the identities of the killers. Which count, Red wondered, related to the man hiding in the closet? Had Wilbarth found a secret witness, perhaps some drover who, like Herrington, had been given a long count by Brayton and split the overpayment with the agent? Or had Wilbarth turned up one of the passengers on that fateful trip who had recognized Schaeffer's assassin? Red doubted that the latter was true. He himself had talked to the brakeman and the handful of passengers who were on the car that night. They were unanimous in saying that they could see nothing out in the night from inside the lamplit coach.

Did the fact that Wilbarth had hidden the person in his closet mean that he knew Red would recognize him if he saw him? Possibly. On the other hand, it might be a stranger whose identity and description had to be kept secret for his own safety.

Well, there was only one thing to do, Red decided. It involved the legwork he both hated and loved — hated because it took effort, and loved because there here always surprises in store.

He rose now, took his hat, went out, and, in the chill morning, headed for Main Street. Once there, he turned and headed for the Prairie House, silently cursing the trouble Wilbarth was putting him to. He knew Wilbarth was only getting even with him for the editorial riding Red had given him ever since Schaeffer's death. Red had a deep distrust of all politicians, no matter what their party, and since Wilbarth was a political appointee, he was fair game.

On the two blocks between the Grandview and the brick-and-stone Prairie House, Red spoke to a dozen people. Half of them coldly returned his greeting, and the rest managed to be looking in store windows or across the street when he passed them. At least two men he knew managed to find a break in the long tie rail where they could cross the street to avoid him. He was used to this, and didn't care.

The Prairie House hack was neither at the front entrance nor at the side entrance, and Red wondered at this. The morning trains to Primrose and to the north had both pulled out some time ago, and the familiar green hotel hack should have been pulled up at one of the entrances.

Red crossed the big empty lobby, circled a huge potted plant before the desk, and spoke to the elderly clerk.

"Morning, Russ. Where's the hack?"

The clerk looked at him distastefully. "The hack is for hotel patrons only, Red."

"Hell, I know that. I want to talk with Steve."

"When he's done taking passengers to the train and it's a nice day, he always washes down the hack. You'll find him out in back."

Red didn't bother to thank him, and left by the side entrance. He found Steve Lister, the hack driver, just where the clerk had told him he would. Coatless, sleeves rolled up, Steve was sponging the spokes of a rear wheel when Red halted beside him.

"What're you doing that for, Steve? It ain't rained for a week."

"Dust," the hack driver said curtly.

Steve was past middle age, a burly man who had been with the hotel since it was built, when the state was still a territory.

"Got a minute, Steve?" Red asked. Steve reluctantly tossed the sponge in the bucket and even more reluctantly came erect.

"I'm trying to find out the name of a man," Red continued. "Don't know what he looks like, how old he is, or where he comes from. You met both trains last night, didn't you?"

"Always do," Lister said coldly. He had a rough, squarish face that was not good at masking his feelings, and now it reflected not only dislike but irritability.

"Who'd you bring in from the early train?"

"Four strangers. Their names are on the register."

"How many did you bring here from the Primrose train?"

"Five. Two of them I know, and so do you. The names of the others will be on the register, like I said."

"Then the last seven names on the register that I don't know will be everyone you brought in last night?"

Steve was momentarily puzzled, but when he followed Red's reasoning, he nodded. "Unless somebody come in after them. Ask Russ. And you better make that the last eight names."

"How's that?" Red asked.

"Fellow give me his saddle and blanket roll and told me he'd walk."

Red came alert now. "What'd he look like, Steve?"

Steve said promptly, "About thirty, cowboy, but clean, over six feet tall, wore a brown duck jacket."

Red eyed him thoughtfully, then said, "Sure you aren't making that up, Steve? It was night, the platform was dark, and unless he came close to your carriage lantern, you couldn't see him that good."

"That's right," Steve said. "But I seen him again at the depot this morning, at the first train."

"With a saddle and blanket roll?"

"Come to think of it, no," Steve said, puzzlement in his face. "Still, he could have throwed his stuff on the seat to hold it, then come outside again. You see, I never took him in the hack. He must have walked again."

Still suspicious, Red said, "Funny you'd notice him that much, Steve. Why did you?"

Steve frowned. "I dunno rightly. He just had a 'go to hell' look in his eyes."

"He was mean-looking, is that it?"

"No, that ain't it," Steve said flatly. "He just looked like he owned as much of the world as he wanted."

"Arrogant?"

Steve shook his head. "I don't know that word, Red."

Red pulled a cigar from the breast pocket of his coat and extended it to Steve, who shook his head, saying, "I don't smoke and you shouldn't, either."

"Don't preach to me," Red snarled. "Save it for your Sunday school boys."

Now Red backtracked to the lobby, and again faced the clerk. "Russ, give me a look at your register, will you?"

"Ain't supposed to." Russ's voice was firm.

Red folded his arms, leaned them on the counter, and regarded Russ almost with pity. "Think a minute, Russ. Do I have to get the sheriff and bring him down here and have him watch me while I look at the register? He won't thank you for that trip. He'll think you're an idiot."

"You looking for a criminal?"

"I am. Now let's look at the register."

Reluctantly the clerk shoved the big register toward him.

"Anybody check in this morning?" Red asked, as he scanned the register.

"Nope."

Steve had been right. Red knew two of the last eight names.

"Who checked out for the morning trains?"

Russ turned the register so he could read the names. "That one and that one." He put his finger on two of the signatures.

"Which train?" Russ asked.

"Primrose."

"None of them for the last train?" Red asked.

Russ shook his head. Red straightened up and asked mildly, "You wouldn't have a saddle and blanket roll that Steve brought in last night, would you?"

Russ pointed under the desk. "Right here."

Red felt a rush of excitement as he walked around the end of the counter. Beneath it were a worn saddle and a blanket roll. Kneeling now, Red dragged out the blanket roll.

"Watch me, Russ. Make sure I don't take anything."

He untied the thongs that held the blankets, and unrolled them on the floor. Two calico shirts, a neckerchief, a pair of spurs, and some clean socks were all the blanket roll held. Red restored them exactly the way he had found them. The blanket re-rolled, Red rose now, feeling a curious sense of anticipation. This surely had to be the gear of the man who had hid in Wilbarth's closet last night. If it wasn't, why had it been left unclaimed? There was only one reason for the saddle and blanket roll to be there: the man hadn't wanted to be seen claiming them.

"All right, Russ. Thanks."

As Red walked around the counter, Russ asked, "What did this fellow do?"

"Killed his wife," Red said carelessly, and headed through the lobby for the street. Once there, he turned toward the station, some ten blocks away. The morning was warming a little, but Red didn't notice it. He didn't even notice the people he met, nor did he speak to them. Once out of the few blocks of business district, Red ran out of plank walk and took to the road.

The depot platform was empty, and Red headed directly for the ticket office inside. The agent had heard him approach, Red knew, but in the fashion of all railroaders, he took his time in getting up to the window.

"Hi, Perry."

"Going someplace, Red?"

"No. How good's your memory, Perry?"

"Not good."

"I'll describe a man that bought a ticket for the early train this morning. See if you can remember where he bought the ticket to."

He went on to give Steve's excellent description of the man, and Perry frowned thoughtfully behind his steel-rimmed glasses as he listened. When Red was finished, Perry nodded.

"I remember. He bought a ticket to Boundary."

"You wouldn't know his name, would you?"

"How could I?" Perry asked.

"That's the trouble with you railroads," Red said in

happy malice. "You just don't care who travels with you."

Red moved over to one of the empty benches and pulled out a cigar, which he clamped in his mouth but did not bother to light, and sat down. What had he learned this morning? That a young man whom Wilbarth had considered worth hiding last night was now on his way to Boundary, which meant, in all probability, the agency. Was Wilbarth trying to shore up the government's case against Con Brayton, hunting new evidence to be used in the trial? And why the secrecy? Maybe Wilbarth had been speaking the truth last night, when he had implied that if the man was identified in the *Times*, he might be killed like Schaeffer.

More importantly, was it worth a story in the *Times*? It would have to be one of those stories that began with 'Rumor has it . . .' He could go on to say that an unidentified man had had a secret night conference with the marshal, and the following morning entrained for Boundary and the reservation. Was new evidence being unearthed for use in the trial of Brayton and Herrington?

Red knew the value of such rumor stories. They invariably infuriated the office-holder mentioned, and sometimes his angry denials could be revealing. Predictably, such a story would anger Wilbarth, but he doubted whether the marshal could be taunted into any damning revelations.

Or he could print a story headlined "Who *is* This Man?" and give Steve's description, plus the destination of the mystery man's train trip. He could make a kind of contest out of it, offering a small reward to anyone who could identify him.

Reluctantly, Red rejected both ideas. Any move now would be premature. And when it came right down to it, whose side was he on, the government's or Brayton and Herrington's? Red instinctively loathed all authority and those who held it, but he conceded that some form of authority was necessary. At the same time, he secretly admired the swindle by Brayton and Herrington of the government. It took the kind of large-scale gall that he wished he himself possessed. Not that he condoned murder to cover the swindle; it was just that two smart men had deceived a stupid government. Well, then, whose side should he be on? Burley Hammond, who owned Consolidated Mining & Milling and also owned Red — had told him he wasn't interested in the case. It was a federal matter and not a state one. If it had been just the opposite and Governor Halsey were involved, he would have ordered Red to go all-out against the state government. Therefore, there was no urgency about identifying the mystery man.

Still, Red wasn't going to let it drop. The mystery man had come in from Primrose, the end of the line for passenger travel. He'd write Bill Harness today, giving him the man's description, and ask him to try and identify the stranger. If he wrote Bill, the letter would have to be accompanied by an overdue check. Red sighed, rose from the station bench, and headed back for the office.

Ten

When Steve Lister finished washing down the hack, he drove the team around to the Main Street entrance of the Prairie House and went inside. Red had been gone only minutes when Steve suddenly remembered that he had seen the man Red wanted to identify some days ago. It was last Sunday, in fact, when a man alighting from the train from the north had told him to take his saddle and blanket roll in the hack, and that he would walk. He remembered it very well because the hack was so crowded that Jimmy Barth, the state senator and a resident guest of the hotel during the legislature session, had sat in the front seat next to him. He could place the day because Jimmy spent each weekend up state with his family, returning on the Sunday-night train to be in time for the Monday session of the legislature.

More out of curiosity than real interest, Steve strolled up to the desk under the indifferent eyes of Russ. Steve disliked Russ, who loved to bang the bell and order him to take out the guest's luggage, in the tone of voice a plantation owner would use in speaking to his slave in the days before the War. Steve now halted before the register and leafed back to last Sunday night's registrations. The man's name would probably be the last on the Sunday list, for at nine o'clock, when he'd gone off duty, the saddle and blanket roll were still behind the desk. Looking at the register, he saw that the name Sam Kennery was the last registration for Sunday night.

Steve went over to his customary chair, against the wall near the front of the lobby, and sat down. Should he tell Red Macandy he knew the man's name? He disliked Red, as did most people who knew him, and he had no reason to do him a favor. Besides, Red had offered him a cigar when everybody in town knew that Steve hated tobacco as he hated the devil. Indeed, he was famous for his lay sermons against the Wicked Weed at his church. He judged Red's offer of a cigar as an insulting gesture of contempt toward him and his beliefs. No, he was going to keep the name Sam Kennery to himself.

Eleven

Following Marshal Wilbarth's instructions to the letter, Anse Newford went aboard the train first and took a front seat, while Sam, boarding last, took a rear seat. The ride across the sere October prairie was a dull one. In late morning they stopped at the drab coal mining town of River Valley for a half-hour layover, and the passengers flocked into a grimy cafe across from the depot for a quick meal. Here, Anse put several stools between himself and Sam.

It was early afternoon when they pulled in for the water stop at Long Reach, and the brakeman came through the car with his usual message that this was only a water stop. When he was gone, Sam rose and went out on the car's platform, where he descended to the lowest step and looked at the bleak prairie that ended against the near mountains. This was the spot where Schaeffer had been killed and Newford had lost an eye. Sam wondered what Newford was thinking right now, and it was not difficult to guess. When he went back to his seat, a brakeman standing near him was discussing the shooting in the prideful tone of a man who had witnessed murder. Either the brakeman was an unthinking clod, or he hadn't recognized Newford, because his description was graphic and bloody. Newford, Sam noticed, did not turn around like the other passengers to hear the brakeman's description of that fateful night.

Once through the timbered pass, they were soon on the prairie again, and it was late afternoon when the train screeched to a halt as the brakeman intoned "Boundary, Boundary. All Boundary passengers off."

Sam was first off, and he looked about him at this bleak, dead prairie. Fifty yards from the track, across a dusty road, was a low adobe building. A badly painted sign above the entrance proclaimed it *McCook's Trading Post*. A smaller sign below it said *Liquor*. Set apart from the post was a small log house backed by a large corral. A team hitched to a buckboard with tandem seats was tied alongside two Indian ponies at the hitch rail, and Sam supposed this was the stage to the agency.

He moved off toward the trading post now, and he could hear footfalls behind him. That would be Anse, but Sam did not look back.

The interior of the trading post was dark and cool, and smelled of untanned hides and coal oil. It was a shabby, single room whose meager shelves held denim pants, socks, bolts of dress goods, and a good supply of navy blue blankets. In a nail keg were a couple of dozen axe handles, and above them was a line of shiny new lanterns, hanging from nails on the wall. Three barrels against the left wall held dried apples, beans, and black jerky. The right wall was taken up by a stained and grimy plank bar resting on sawhorses. Beyond it, toward the rear, were the stinking hides. A fat squaw, her blanket loose around her shoulders, was studying the bolts of dress goods, not touching them. An Indian, probably her husband, was squatting alongside the barrel of jerky, his back against the wall. He wore buckskin leggings and moccasins and a cotton shirt, tails out. Neither he nor the woman even glanced at Sam.

Behind the bar, a middle-aged man was pouring whiskey from a gallon jug into a row of pint bottles, and as Sam moved over to him he heard Newford enter the post.

At the bar, Sam halted and said, "Mr. McCook?" The man nodded without taking his eyes off his pouring. Under a buttonless vest, he wore a dirty blue striped shirt with no collar, and Sam noted that the brass collar button of the shirt had stained McCook's neck a faint green. The man had needed a shave for the past month. Sam reached in his jacket pocket for Brayton's letter, and then, out of the corner of his eye he saw Newford come up to the bar. Sam turned and looked at him. "Go ahead. This can wait," he said.

Newford nodded his thanks and said to McCook, "When does the stage leave?"

McCook set down his jug and, without looking at them, turned his head toward the rear of the room and yelled, "Barney!" Only then did he look at Newford, and Sam noted that his pale eyes were red-rimmed and bloodshot.

"That'll be five dollars," McCook said to Newford.

"For a five-mile ride?" Newford asked in disbelief.

McCook shrugged. "It's a hot walk, but go ahead."

Wordlessly, Newford reached in his pocket for the money. As he did so, a young Indian dressed in cotton shirt and Levi's came out of the back room and passed him on his way to the door.

Lazily, McCook moved up to Newford, who tossed a gold coin on the table. "You got a good thing going for you in that stage," Newford said dryly.

"Yup, but it's almost always government expense money. They can afford it."

Newford got his change and walked out, and now McCook turned his attention to Sam.

"Got a letter for you," Sam said, and extended Brayton's letter in its envelope. McCook read it and said, "Yup. What can I do for you?"

"I need a horse, a saddle, blankets, and a couple quarts of whiskey."

McCook nodded. "Take the gray, out in the corral. Saddle's in the shed. I'd do it myself, but these damned Injuns would steal the store if I went outside. I'll have your blankets and whiskey ready for you."

Sam went out through the back door and headed for the open-faced shed behind the house. He found the saddle in the corner of the shed, and lugged it over to the corral, which held three horses. Taking the rope from the saddle, he moved into the corral. The gray eyed him curiously, but stood perfectly still as Sam put the loop around his neck and led him out to be saddled. Afterwards, Sam lengthened the stirrups and led the horse to the rear door of the post. In his absence, McCook had wrapped the two quarts of whiskey in the two new navy blue blankets. Both ends of the blanket roll were tied, separating the bottles. He waited in the doorway as Sam tramped up.

"I might have to keep this horse awhile," Sam said.

"Don't matter. Con will pay." He frowned. "Can I

ask where you're going?"

"No."

"Well, I hope you get there," McCook said. He turned and disappeared inside the post.

As he picked up the agency road, Sam noted that the buckboard was already gone, and now, headed north on the dusty road, he realized he was entering Brayton's domain. Nothing marked its boundary, but when he saw the first cluster of tepees, he knew he was on the reservation. The faraway children playing among the tepees stopped their game long enough to watch him, and Sam knew from long experience that the news of his presence here would precede him by moccasin telegraph. It might even reach Joe Potatoes, who, though not expecting him, might want to look at him out of simple curiosity.

It was bleak country he rode through, but he could not suppress a sense of expectancy. If Joe Potatoes could be persuaded to talk, then his trip back to Primrose would be the purest pleasure. He wondered idly how Brayton and Herrington would take their arrest and the news of his betrayal. He thought he knew how Carnes would take his — not with protest, but with violence.

In the lowering dusk, he saw two mounted Indians coming down the road toward him, but they immediately pulled off it to skirt him. Now, topping a rise, he saw a mass of yellow-leafed cottonwoods far ahead of him, and he guessed that this was the agency. The next rain would wipe out all the color, and winter would soon clamp down on this barren land, he knew. Between him and the cottonwoods were a huge corral and stock pens, where the monthly beef issue took place. This was the place where, with luck, he would take Joe Potatoes, so he and Newford could seize him.

Brayton had never bothered to describe Joe physically, nor had he said whether he was young or old. That was carelessness on his own part, Sam thought wryly — he should have asked. Beyond the trading post were a couple of log warehouses off to the north, and they made up the remainder of the agency buildings. The lamps inside the post had already been lighted against the lowering dusk.

As Sam rode up to the tie rail, he wondered at the number of ponies, and then he remembered the Indian sense of timelessness. Where a white family man would come home at the end of his work day for supper and rest, the Indian ate when he was hungry and kept his own hours. The pattern of Indian life, Sam thought, was no pattern at all. Dismounting, Sam tied his horse, then climbed the two steps and tramped across the veranda to the open door, and halted just inside it. The post was one huge room, its rafters supported by widely spaced log pillars. There was a counter running the depth of the room on his right, and a similar one on his left, and behind these counters, on shelves, were stacked trading goods, clothing, and hardware. From the pillars hung tangles of harness and rope. A few new saddles were in evidence, and Sam guessed these were a hard item to move in a land whose people rode bare back. It seemed to be a room filled with many items, from the black Stetsons coming into favor with the Indians to moccasins made by the Indians for sale to those of them who had no women to make them. Three Indians who had come in to escape the evening chill had seated themselves on the counter to the left. Behind the right counter, to the rear, was a towheaded young man conversing with an Indian man in his own language. When the Indian moved off to join his friends at the counter, the young man looked up, saw Sam, and moved toward him behind the counter.

Sam came over to the counter and halted under an overhead kerosene lamp.

"If you're looking for Dad, he's eating supper," the young man said pleasantly. He could have been nineteen, and he had the unweathered and worried-looking face of a person who spent his time indoors, concerning himself with money.

"Don't need him," Sam said cheerfully. "You can likely tell me. Where could a man put up here and get something to eat?"

"The agency, sir. The agent's not here now, but his housekeeper will feed you. There's a sleeping room up in the attic." He added with a faint smile, "I heard you were on your way."

Sam nodded, and smiled too. "I figured you would."

"You can put McCook's horse in the corral behind the agency," the young man said, and then added, almost with embarrassment, "If you're broke, you can sleep here on the floor tonight after I shoo the Indians out."

"What time would that be?" Sam asked curiously.

"Nine o'clock."

"And how did you know I'm riding McCook's horse?"

The young man used a wholly Indian gesture. He literally pointed with his lifted chin to the group of Indians across the store. "One of them told me."

"No secrets around here," Sam observed.

"No, sir."

"Give me five pounds of jerky and five pounds of flour and some matches, will you?"

The young man left to fill his order, and Sam strolled back to the door. If they knew he was coming and they knew he was riding McCook's horse, they might also know he had two quarts of whiskey in his blanket roll. It was not quite fully dark, and he saw that lamps were now lighted in the agency. When the young man brought him the supplies in a muslin flour sack, Sam paid him and thanked him, then went out and mounted his horse.

Sam rode over to the agency barn and turned his horse out into the tiny corral adjoining the barn. By matchlight he found a feedbag and the oats in the barn, and fed his horse. He loosened the saddle cinch, but left the gray saddled.

It was completely dark when he rounded the house with his blanket roll and supply sack, skirted the dark office, and mounted the steps to the small porch.

The door was opened by a gaunt Indian woman wearing a prim, long-sleeved cotton dress. "Can I put up here for the night?" Sam asked. As he was talking, he saw, beyond her shoulder, Anse Newford and a half-breed Indian eating at the big dining table in the room.

She said, "Come in," and Sam stepped past her. Newford and the breed regarded him curiously, and Sam bade them a civil good evening. The Indian woman skirted the table, drew out a chair alongside Newford. and vanished into the kitchen.

"There's a washbench out by the back door," Newford said.

"Does the woman speak English?" Sam asked of the breed.

"Not speak good but she understand good," the half-breed said. He was, Sam supposed, an agency employee of Brayton's.

Sam dumped his blanket roll in a corner, but kept the sack of supplies, threw his hat on his blanket roll, and went out into the kitchen. The Indian woman was at the stove, and when she heard Sam approach, she turned.

"Can you make me up some bannock tonight? I'll be leaving very early." He extended the sack and the woman opened it and looked and felt inside. Withdrawing her hand, she held up one finger and said, "Hour."

Sam went out the door, found the washbench, washed up, and came back through the kitchen, followed by the woman with a platter of steaks.

The supper was good and, oddly enough, so was the company. The breed was bursting with curiosity to know Sam's business on the reservation, but all Sam would say was that he was passing through.

"You buy McCook's horse?" the breed asked craftily.

"I'll be back," Sam said. Then he and Newford

matched lies for the breed's benefit. Newford said he was a deputy marshal requested to come here by Brayton to investigate whiskey smuggling. There had been some trouble with drunken Indians on the reservation. The breed said there was always trouble with drunken Indians. Newford said he'd hired a horse from Buckhalter, the post trader, and was heading out tomorrow. Sam said he himself was a horse buyer, shortcutting through the reservation to pick up a herd at Lansing. He'd drive the horses back south, dropping off McCook's gray on the way.

Finished with his supper, the breed rose and said he would see Newford in the morning, but Newford said he would be long gone by daylight. The breed went out and Newford, hearing the Indian cook clattering pans in the kitchen, judged that it was safe to talk.

"I found our man, Sam," Newford said quietly.

"How?"

"Easy. I asked the trader who the worst drunks were, and he pointed out Joe Potatoes as one of 'em. He was still at the post when I left."

"Then it's tonight?"

Newford nodded. "No sense waiting if we find him. You leave here first and tie your horse behind the post, then go inside and buy a bandanna or something. If Joe is still there, I'll go up and talk to him. When I leave, pick him up any way you can. I'll head for the corrals. Did you notice that cedar-stake branding corral when you came by?" At Sam's nod, Newford said, "That'll be the place. Talk loud enough so I can pick up your voice. He's big and —"

"Watch it," Sam cut in.

On the heels of his warning, the Indian cook came into the room and placed Sam's flour sack, with the still-warm soda bread in it, on the table. Sam rose, held out his hand, and said to Newford. "If I don't see you again, good luck."

Newford, still seated, extended his hand and said, "Luck to you."

Sam turned to the Indian woman. "How much do I owe you?"

"You want bed?"

When Sam shook his head, she said. "Half-dollar supper, quarter-dollar cook." Sam paid her and walked to his blanket roll with the sack. He picked up the blanket-roll, put on his hat, paused at the door, and said, "So long," and stepped out into the night.

At the corral, he stored his provisions in a saddlebag and tied on his blanket roll, but not before undoing a thong and removing a bottle, which he placed in the other saddlebag. Then, he cinched up and rode up toward the post. Circling it in the darkness, he tied his horse at a grindstone his mount had swerved to avoid, went back to the front veranda, and entered the store.

There were still a few Indians around, but they had all moved off the veranda to escape the chill night air. The same young man was behind the counter, and for all Sam knew, the same Indians were seated on the other counter.

Sam asked the young clerk for a bandanna, and was trying on gloves when Newford entered. Newford cut to the counter where the Indians were seated. Sam watched him halt before them and say something to them, after which the Indian in the middle slid off the counter. Newford moved a few paces to the rear of the store and the Indian followed. He was, Sam saw, a big and burly young man with a blanket tucked into the waistband of his filthy Levi's. His hair was braided tightly and fell below each shoulder in front. Newford, with a scowl on his face, talked with him for a few minutes and then shook his head, left him, and went out the front door.

Sam found a pair of gloves he liked, rammed them in his hip pocket, and paid his bill. Then, he moved over to the other counter where Joe, standing now, was evidently recounting his conversation with Newford. The Indians laughed at something he said, and then, as Sam approached, they fell silent. Joe turned to look at the reason for their silence, and Sam halted beside him.

"Come outside, Joe," Sam said pleasantly.

For a moment, Sam thought Joe was going to pretend ignorance of English, but either his curiosity or the realization that Sam had seen him talking with Newford seemed to change his mind. Sam headed for the door, hearing the whispering of Joe's moccasins on the floor behind him.

Sam stepped out onto the veranda and halted in the dim light cast by the overhead lamps inside. Joe Potatoes halted too, and Sam studied the broad, sullen, suspicious, and sick-looking face.

"Brayton sent me," Sam said finally.
"You got money?"
Sam nodded. "Whiskey too."
"Where?"
"You got a horse?" Joe looked puzzled, then slowly

turned his head and pointed with his chin to one of the horses at the tie rail.

"Wait there." Sam turned to head for the steps.

"You pay," Joe said.

Sam halted. "Not here," he said flatly, and went down the steps.

When he had retrieved his horse and circled back, Joe was already mounted on his Indian pony, and Sam reined in beside him. "We'll ride down to the issue corral, Joe."

"No. Too far."

"That's where the rest of the whiskey is, Joe. I hid it."

Sam reached back and opened the flap of the saddlebag and took out a bottle of whiskey. He held it out to Joe, saying, "Here's a start, Joe." Joe reached for the bottle and Sam heard him swiftly wrench out the cork. He heard a gurgle and then an explosion of breath as the whiskey went down.

"Now let's go, Joe." Dutifully, Joe fell in behind him, and as Sam's eyes became accustomed to the darkness, he saw Joe riding beside him, the bottle held on his thigh and pointing skyward as if it might have been a rifle.

They had not even passed the agency before Joe took his second drink. On the half-mile ride between his third and fourth drink, Joe asked, "How much money?"

"Brayton didn't say, Joe."

"How much whiskey?"

"Ten bottles," Sam lied. He heard Joe's grunt of satisfaction.

When they came to the issue corrals, Joe halted his pony. "Where?" he asked.

"At the branding corral," Sam said. They skirted the bigger holding corral in silence, and approached the branding corral. Remembering Anse Newford's admonition to make himself heard, Sam said, "How you going to pack all this booze, Joe?"

"I hide it again," Joe said.

"You mean you don't trust me, Joe?" Sam said, just to make a noise.

"No take chances," Joe replied flatly.

Sam picked a spot at random, dismounted, and then struck a match.

"What you lost?" Joe asked.

Sam held the match high in the still night and said, "I marked it by a rock against the posts, Joe. Help me look." The match died.

Joe slipped off his pony, bottle still in hand, and began walking in the opposite direction to that which Sam had taken. Sam reversed directions to put himself between Joe and his pony. As quietly as he could, he moved up behind Joe, wondering whether he should wait for Anse or take Joe alone.

The decision was made for him, for Joe, hearing Sam behind him, turned. Sam lifted his gun and said quietly, "All right, Joe, you're under arrest. I've got a gun on you. Drop that bottle."

Joe exploded toward him, raising his bottle like a club. Sam knew that this Indian would do them no good dead. Instinctively he raised his right arm, gun in hand, to ward off Joe's blow. When it came slashing down, the bottle hit his sixgun and smashed, showering him with broken glass and blinding him with raw whiskey. Sam pivoted aside. Through tears flushed into his eyes by the whiskey, he saw that Joe still had the jagged-edged neck of the bottle in his hand. Joe's lunge turned into a run, then, as he raced for his horse only a few yards away, Sam exploded into motion, aiming to put himself between Joe and the horse. Then, out of the deep darkness of the close-set corral poles, a figure hurtled into Joe, sending him reeling in Sam's direction. In mid-stride, Sam raised his gun and brought it down on Joe's skull. It was a hard blow, audible in spite of the cushioning effect of Joe's black Stetson. Joe never caught his balance; he simply folded to the ground on his back. Sam put a foot on Joe's right arm; then, with his other foot, he kicked the jagged glass out of Joe's limp fist.

Newford loomed out of the night, leading Joe's Indian pony, and halted by Sam, who was now wiping his face with his jacket sleeve. Kneeling by Joe, Anse said, "There should be a knife." Presently he came up with it, then rose. "Man, you smell like a saloon," he observed.

"I'd rather have that stuff on me than in me," Sam said wryly. Then he added, "Let's get him loaded while he's still out. Where's your horse?"

"With yours."

Sam moved off into the night, found the horses, and returned with them. Anse had rolled Joe over on his face and handcuffed his arms behind his back. Now he and Sam picked up Joe's slack body and wrestled it astride the pony. With Anse's rope, they tied Joe's feet together under the horse's belly, and Sam's rope they looped over the pony's head for a lead.

Only then did Sam draw out his newly bought bandanna and wipe the whiskey from his eyes and face.

"Will you lead or will I, Anse?"

"I'd better. We head northeast for a low pass. The boss drew a map for me."

Sam said grimly, "Then let's move. Nothing happens in daylight that these Indians don't know about. Let's see if we can get out of their way tonight."

Suddenly, Joe's Indian pony snorted and reared, and at the same time tried to wheel. Anse, holding the lead rope, tightened his hold on it, and Sam, knowing the horse would run when all four feet were on the ground again, lunged in behind Anse and seized the tail of the rope. Predictably, the horse's forequarters came down as Joe shouted a command in Indian.

Both Anse and Sam dug in their heels as the pony lunged against the rope. They had to give a little before the horse was choked down; it turned and came toward them to slack the rope.

"That was close, but not good enough, Joe," Sam called.

Joe, now that his trick of feigning unconsciousness had failed, straightened up, but did not speak. Anse took the lead rope, moved over to his horse, dallied the rope around the horn, and swung into the saddle. Sam mounted his gray and the three men moved off into the cold night, heading northeast for the mountains that blacked out the stars on the jagged horizon.

By daylight they traveled through the foothills, and

at dawn were in the timber. When they picked up a creek, they followed it until it cut through a grassy park. Here Joe was unloaded and seated against a tree, where his legs were tied and his arms were freed. While Anse picketed the three horses, Sam brought out a bannock and some jerky. Joe watched all this with stolid indifference. When Anse returned to the camp, his boots were glistening with dew; he knelt at the stream, had his drink, and then came up to Joe.

Sam had already divided the bannock and jerky, and put Joe's portion within reach of him. Anse looked at it, and then at Joe. "Better eat it, Joe," Anse said. "It won't taste so good when I tell you why you're under arrest." He pause "Remember Schaeffer? You worked for him."

Joe might have been deaf, for all the expression in his face and eyes.

"I can't promise you this, Joe, but I think they'll hang you for his murder."

Now he indicated Sam. "This is Deputy U.S. Marshal Sam Kennery, Joe. Maybe he wants to say something to you."

Anse glanced at Sam, who was watching the Indian.

"Only this, Joe," Sam said quietly. "Try to escape and one or both of us will shoot you in the legs. It won't be so bad if we don't break a bone. Still, they'll hang a man even with a broken leg. It's just a little uncomfortable, waiting."

Joe didn't bother to look at him.

Anse took a paper from his jacket pocket, unfolded it, and held it down for Joe to look at. "Let's make it legal, Joe. This is a warrant for your arrest on suspicion of murder and complicity in murder. Now you've seen it, and I'll so testify at your trial."

Joe didn't even look at the warrant.

They ate and rested while their horses grazed, and afterwards rode on, using game trails through the timber when they could, and staying far away from the stage road that crossed the mountains.

That night they camped by a stream in the timber, built a fire this time, and ate the same things they had eaten that morning. Sam's extra blankets were used for Joe, who slept with arms handcuffed and feet bound. Sam took the watch till midnight, and Anse took the shift till dawn.

At midmorning of the following day they crossed the pass, which held a foot of snow between the shouldering peaks on either side. They met no one and, as far as Sam could tell after circling their back-trail twice that morning, were not followed. Maybe Brayton had been right when he said nobody knew or cared enough about Joe to be concerned by his disappearance.

It was close to dark when they broke out of the timber where a broad valley lay below them. A cluster of distant lights told Sam by their number that this was not a ranch, but a sizeable settlement. It would, of course, be Crater, named for its location in the vast hollow of a long-extinct volcano. Minutes later they picked up the road they had avoided so carefully the past two days.

It was full night when they picked up Crater's main

street. As far as Sam could tell, most of the buildings were built of logs from the surrounding mountains, although an occasional frame structure testified to the presence of a nearby sawmill. It was a dark and gloomy-looking town this night, with only the saloons and a big frame hotel at the four main corners lighted.

As they passed the hotel, Sam said, "Shall I check here for Wilbarth?"

"He said he'd be at the courthouse," Anse said, then added, "We got him this far. Let's get him behind jail bars."

Sam saw Joe studying the town. It was almost the first time in two days that he had really paid attention to anyone or anything. The livery stable, with lanterns flanking its archway, marked the end of the business district. There were lamps lighted here and there in the houses and cabins along the way. Sam saw a big building looming up on the left, ahead of them. That would be the courthouse, he guessed, and as they approached it, Sam saw the lamps burning in the near front-corner office of the big frame building. At the tie rail closest to the door they halted, dismounted, and freed Joe's legs. Joe was so stiff that Sam had to heave his leg over the pony's back, and when he hit the ground, his legs wouldn't hold his weight. Anse caught him before he fell, and held him erect while Joe shook one leg and then the other, to free himself from the long ride's stiffness. When he could stand erect unaided, Anse touched his arm and they moved toward the faintly lit stone steps of the courthouse. Joe had set some kind of a record for silence, even for an Indian, Sam thought. He hadn't spoken since his capture two nights ago.

They picked up the cross-corridor, turned left, and saw Wilbarth standing in the doorway of the sheriff's office, silhouetted by the lamp inside. He was wearing a dark suit, his only concession to the amenities expected of a public official. Newford spoke first.

"Here's your man, Wes. You wouldn't know it from him, though."

"Cold ride?"

"Cold enough," Anse said.

Now Wilbarth stepped up, touched Joe's arm, and said, "Step inside."

Joe moved into the room with Wilbarth behind him, and Sam and Anse following the chief marshal. An elderly man rose from the chair facing the desk, which a younger man was leaning against. Both men were dressed in denim pants and wool shirts, and Wilbarth introduced them as Sheriff Ritter and his deputy, Byron Packer. Sam and Anse shook hands with the two men, and then Packer moved over toward Joe. "Who's got the handcuff key?" he asked.

Anse gave it to him, and Packer paused by Joe and pointed to a railed-off staircase on the south side of the big room.

"Downstairs, Joe."

Without a look at any of them, Joe vanished down the steps, Packer behind him.

Now Wilbarth looked at Sam and Anse. "A quiet one?" Wilbarth asked.

"He hasn't said a word, Wes. I mean that literally. Not a word."

"Kennery, how'd you get him?"

Sam told him how Anse had pointed out to him, and told of their capture of him and his attempt to break away. As he was finishing, Packer came up the stairs, took his jacket and hat from a nail on the wall, and waited until Sam was finished. Then he said to Sheriff Ritter, "I'll get some grub for him."

Wilbarth said to Anse and Sam, "That's what you two better do for yourselves."

The three men moved out of the office, and Ritter observed wryly to Wilbarth, "I'll trade you one of my deputies for one of yours."

Wilbarth smiled faintly and moved over to the chair by the desk. "He after your job, Al?" he asked, sitting down.

"Of course," Ritter said. "Behind my back, he's saying I ought to be put out to pasture."

They began reminiscing about their long-ago association, and were still at it when Packer came in with the tray holding Joe's supper. Wilbarth gave Joe fifteen minutes to eat it, and then broke off their yarning. Rising, he said, "Let's go see him, Al."

In the three-cell jail below, they found Packer taking out the tray from Joe's cell, which contained two cots. Finished with his meal, Joe was lying down and didn't even look at them. Sheriff Ritter picked up Packer's chair and carried it to the cell, indicating that the cot was for Wilbarth.

The marshal began matter-of-factly, "Joe, Brayton told us you understand English and speak it, so don't pretend you don't know what I'm talking about. First, I'll repeat the charges filed against you and tell you what your rights are."

He proceeded to do just that, telling him that he could be legally held for forty-eight hours on each charge, of which there were two; he was entitled to legal counsel, and there were two lawyers in this county seat town; if his lawyer so demanded, he could be freed on bond after ninety-six hours had passed; the court would undoubtedly place a bond on him of an amount that he could not possibly raise, therefore, to all intents and purposes, he was a prisoner from now on, with no hope of being freed until trial. Unless he wanted to spend the winter here, he had better talk. Specifically, he had better answer the questions Wilbarth was about to put to him. Joe listened as would a deaf man who, hearing nothing, showed no reaction to the words spoken to him.

Wilbarth continued, "Joe, one of those men who brought you in — the tall one — was paid a hundred dollars by Brayton to go up to the reservation and kill you. Brayton even told him why he wanted you killed. You and another man, on the night of September the thirteenth, waited for the train to stop at the Long Reach water tank. You rode alongside the passenger car until you found Mort Schaeffer, then you shotgunned him through a window."

There was a racket on the stairs, and Wilbarth waited till he saw Packer step into sight and halt in the doorway almost directly under the overhead lamp.

Wilbarth continued, "We have proof that Brayton paid you and the other man to kill Schaeffer. We also know you've been blackmailing Brayton. Do you know what blackmail is, Joe?" Joe was looking at the ceiling and didn't answer. "You're asking Brayton for whiskey money, Joe, or else you'll turn him over to the law. That's why he wanted you killed. Now, we don't think you killed Schaeffer, Joe; we think the other man did. What was his name?" Suddenly Wilbarth rose and moved over to Joe's cot.

Joe was asleep.

Again there was the sound of footfalls on the stairs, and Sam and Anse emerged from the stairwell and halted under the corner lamp. Wilbarth glowered at them, and then said to Packer, "Wake him up and keep him awake." Packer came into the cell and over to Joe and shook him. Joe opened his eyes and looked past Packer at the ceiling. Wilbarth, to Sam's surprise, was not angry. He was studying the wall of the cell, which held a window, and then his glance shifted to the other two cells, which also had windows. Packer and Sheriff Ritter watched him, puzzled.

Wilbarth turned to Ritter and said, "Will those two windows open?"

"Yes. It gets pretty hot here in the summer, Wes."

"Packer, open them now. But first take the blankets from his cot." Wilbarth looked past Ritter. "Anse, can you stay awake until midnight, when Sam can spell you?"

"Sure. Spell me to do what?"

"Joe likes to sleep, so we'll see how he does without any," Wilbarth said dryly. "I want one man in the cell, without a gun. That'll be you for tonight, Packer. You got any warm clothes here?"

"A sheepskin up in the office."

"Go get it," Wilbarth said. "A second man — that'll be you until midnight, Anse, and Sam till dawn

— will sit in the corridor, riding shotgun. I've got a mackinaw you can wear. Whoever's in the cell with Joe will keep him awake if the cold doesn't. Now, gentlemen, we'll ventilate this place."

Packer took both of Joe's blankets, which were folded on the foot of the cot, deposited them in the corridor, then opened the cell window, after which he opened the windows in the other two cells. The chill night air, close to freezing, blew into the cell block. Anse borrowed Sam's duck jacket, and Packer went upstairs and returned with a sheepskin. Once Anse had locked Packer in with Joe, he took up his vigil in the corridor. Sam and Wilbarth parted with Sheriff Ritter at the courthouse steps and headed for the hotel in the frosty night.

Twelve

When Billy Foster came into the *Capital Times* office in midmorning, he found Red Macandy in shirtsleeves, seated at the square desk. Billy shrugged out of his coat, hung it on the coat rack, and then moved over to his slot in the desk facing Red. He was seating himself when Red said, "How's Wilbarth this morning? Still on the boil?"

"He's out of town."

Red leaned back in his chair, removed the half-chewed cigar from his mouth, and regarded Billy coldly. His thin saddle of red hair was uncombed this morning and Billy, catching the reek of stale liquor, guessed that Red just possibly hadn't even been to bed last night.

"Where?" Red asked.

"Bailey wouldn't tell me."

"Who's Bailey?"

"Special deputy. He takes messages when they're both out of town."

"Newford gone?"

Billy nodded. "That's right."

"Where?" Red asked bitingly.

"I don't know," Billy said flatly, a show of anger in his voice. "You told me to keep track of Wilbarth, and Bailey wouldn't talk. What am I supposed to do? Read Bailey's mind?"

Red tossed his cigar butt in the ashtray, making it a gesture of utter disgust. "Oh, nothing like that. You're only supposed to earn your wages. You're told that both the marshal and his deputy are out of town. You aren't even curious as to why."

"What good would curiosity do me?" Billy asked hotly. "What am I supposed to do? Throw Bailey down, grab him by the ears, and beat his head on the floor until he talks?"

Red leaned forward now, and said in quiet fury, "That's enough of your lip sonny. Now I'll spell out what you should do, because you're too damned stupid to think of it yourself. Go to Bales' Livery. That's on Main Street. Get a stranger to show you where Main Street is. At Bales', see if the marshal's horse is there. A horse is a four-legged domesticated animal that people ride. If the horse is there, ask if Wilbarth has rented a rig. A rig is something a horse pulls and a man rides in. If Wilbarth didn't hire a rig, you go to the choo-choo depot, sonny. Ask Perry when Newford left and when Wilbarth left. Ask him where they bought tickets to. Write it down, because you're too young to remember. Then ask someone at the depot how to get back to this office. Now get the hell out of here!"

Billy got to his feet, his face white with anger, and stamped over to the coatrack under Red's baleful gaze. His coat on, Billy moved to the door and went out, slamming it behind him with a violence that shook the building.

Red opened the right-hand drawer of his desk, took out a cigar, and jammed it into the corner of his mouth.

He was motionless for a long minute, waiting for his rampaging heart to quiet. That damned kid would kill him yet, he thought bleakly. It was a mistake to allow him to do anything except sweet-talk a bunch of local pants-sellers into advertising their wares in the paper.

His choler now contained, Red thought about the disappearance of both Wilbarth and Newford. Something was up. Was it connected with the man in Wilbarth's closet? That thought caused him to glance at the clock above the file shelf on the right wall. The mail would be up by now, and with any luck there would be a letter from Ben Harness, saying either he could or couldn't identify the man in the closet. His cigar still unlighted, Red stood, put on his coat and hat, and stepped out into the overcast day. There was some weather coming, Red thought, and the prospect of the coming winter depressed him.

Junction City's post office had originally been in a rear corner of Cleveland's Hardware Store on Main Street. As the capital city grew and its mail load increased, it was moved to one of the back storerooms of the store, into which a door was cut that let onto an alley often clogged by freight wagons, drays, and tethered horses. Red threaded his way through the alley traffic and entered the dark post office, where a dozen people, half of them women, were waiting in line before the single window. Red took his place at the end of the line, and it was then that he remembered he hadn't lighted his cigar. He proceeded to do so now, puffing furiously to get the half-wet stogie to burn. The cloud of smoke erupting around him caused two of the women in line to look back at him and ostentatiously cough. Red ignored them. When he received his mail he didn't examine it, knowing by experience that the room was too dark to read in. Leaving the alley, he walked the block to the Prairie House and entered the saloon that opened on its lobby. At the small bar he ordered whiskey, took his glass and bottle to the closest of the three tables, and sat down. After one drink, which was purely medicinal this morning, he looked through his mail. Sure enough, there was an envelope addressed in Ben Harness's impatient handwriting.

>Red,
>   Your check was two dollars short and I can prove it.
>   Yes, I think I know the man you described. He's been hanging around drinking with Brayton and Herrington. As soon as you pay me the money owed, I will telegraph his name to you.
>   Y'r Disob'nt Serv't
>   Ben

Red swore so furiously that the bartender's attention was attracted to him. Morosely, Red had another drink, paid up, then headed for his office.

When he entered it, he saw that Billy Foster had returned. He too had stopped at the post office, probably on his way to the depot, for he was reading a letter that he quickly folded and rammed into his hip pocket. Red shrugged out of his coat, put his hat on the top of the rack, and came over to his desk.

"Well, kid, what have you got for me?" he asked as he sat down.

Billy looked at him with undisguised hatred and said tonelessly, "Wilbarth left yesterday for Crater. Newford left two days before that for Boundary."

Red thought about this for a moment. Then Newford had been on the train with the man in the closet. Any connection there? Surely, if they'd been together, Steve would have mentioned it. Still, both of them were headed for Boundary and presumably the agency.

But what was Wilbarth doing in Crater, which was even north of the agency and the reservation? There must be some connection between the reservation and Crater, but Red couldn't guess what. And how could the man in the closet be a drinking companion of Brayton and Herrington and still be friends with Wilbarth, the man who was going to help prosecute them? There was something funny going on here, Red's instinct told him, but the sum of the parts didn't add up to a recognizable whole. Something was missing and he intended to find out what it was. Reaching in his desk drawer, he drew out an envelope and addressed it to Ben Harness in Primrose. He put inside it three dollars, two of which were the money he owed Ben; the third was to pay for the telegram.

Then, he reached in the bottom drawer and drew out the well-thumbed notebook that contained the names and addresses of perhaps five hundred people in the state, ranging from politicians to madams of sporting houses. In the back of the book was a list of the paper's correspondents. Since the *Capital Times* was the only daily newspaper in the state, and therefore widely read, Red had long ago arranged to have a stringer in the county seat of every county in the state. Usually it was the editor of the weekly newspaper, if the county seat had one. Crater, he remembered, didn't. The name of his stringer in Crater was listed as Martin Flagg. A notation beside the name identified him as the station agent and telegraph operator.

Now Red reached for a sheet of copy paper and scribbled a message:

> Find out U.S. Marshal Wes Wilbarth's business in Crater. Telegraph in detail.
> Red Macandy.

Red folded the paper, and tossed it and the envelope across the desk to Billy. "Send that telegram, Billy, and mail this letter."

"They both cost money," Billy said coldly.

Red swore as he reached again for his wallet.

Thirteen

It was almost noon when Martin Flagg, station agent for the railroad at Crater, heard his call on the telegraph sounder. Picking up a pencil, he pulled a pad toward him and translated the clacking of the sounder into Red Macandy's message to him. Flagg was a heavy, soft, pale man of fifty, with curly — almost kinky — graying hair, who relished the dirty stories exchanged in Morse code among agents down the line. By nature a gregarious man, he had a termagant wife who saw to it that after working hours he was never out of her sight. Accordingly he welcomed any diversion, and Red's telegram promised him one. He knew, of course, that Wilbarth had come in on yesterday's train, but he had no notion of the marshal's business. He acknowledged receipt of the message and signed off.

Leaning back in his chair, he pondered his next move. After the noon meal he would forego his customary nap and go down to the courthouse. Chances were that that old fogey Ritter would be out having his dinner, leaving Byron Packer alone in the office, which was just what he wanted.

Ritter, Flagg reflected, had been sheriff for so long that he acted like the emperor of a tiny kingdom; he was dictatorial, secretive, and senile, only kept in office by a flock of relatives spotted throughout the county. Packer, on the other hand, was a young go-getter who would probably become the county sheriff at next month's election. He would, Flagg judged, be very cooperative with a voter, and Flagg was certainly that.

Flagg rose and put on his coat, overcoat, and hat, threw some wood in the potbellied stove in the waiting room, locked up the station, and tramped through the cool noon to his modest home. At twelve-thirty, almost to the minute, he climbed the courthouse steps and entered the sheriff's office. Sure enough, Packer was seated at the sheriff's desk, writing.

Hearing Flagg enter, he looked up and gave the agent the easy smile of an ambitious politician. "Well, Martin, the train's quit runnin'?"

"Of course," Martin said. "You know they can't run without me."

They both laughed, and Flagg unbuttoned his coat and took a chair beside the desk.

"What can I do for you?" Packer asked.

"Nothing really. I'm just curious. I saw Marshal Wilbarth at the depot yesterday, but I only had time to say hello. What's he doing up here?"

Elbows on the arms of his chair, Packer raised his big, meaty hands and steepled his fingers. Martin's question started a train of thought that was really a list of resentments. Wilbarth and his two deputies had not only taken over the office and jail, but the marshal had treated Packer as a not-very-bright hired hand. Packer had them to thank for a chilly evening and a short night's sleep. He could look forward to the same thing tonight if the Indian didn't talk today. Moreover,

Wilbarth was an old friend of Ritter's, and therefore was in the opposition camp. All three federal men had left him out of their confidence so emphatically that, while he knew the Indian was being held until he named his partner in committing the murder, he did not know the special status of Kennery or the nature of his special assignment. What finally decided him to answer Martin, however, was that Ritter, who should have taken him into his complete confidence, hadn't thought it necessary to do so.

"Why, Wilbarth is up here to question an Injun that Kennery and Newford brought up from the reservation. They think the Injun and another fellow killed Mort Schaeffer. You remember that shotgunning of a passenger car at the Long Reach tank?"

"Yes. Pretty bloody."

"Well, the Injun's not talking," Packer said smugly. "If he was my prisoner, I'd go down to the store and get me an axe handle. He'd talk or there'd be a dead Injun. All they're doing is keeping him awake until he trades some talk for some sleep. They were at him all night and all of today."

"What's this Indian's name?"

Packer shrugged. "They call him Joe."

"Why'd they bring him here? Junction City's got a jail."

"You got me there. Martin. Maybe Wilbarth just wanted to chew the rag with his old friend, Ritter."

Martin frowned pensively, then spread his hands and shrugged. "Doesn't make sense. They could have got the train at Boundary and been in Wilbarth's office that night. Instead, Wilbarth travels all day and the other two cross a mountain range to get here."

That reminded him of his job. "What did you say the names of his deputies are? I'd better write them down."

Packer waited until Flag drew a pencil and paper from his inside pocket, and then told him the names.

"How do you spell Kennery?"

"Ain't seen it spelled, Martin, and he ain't the kind of a man you'd ask."

Flagg made his guess and wrote it down. Afterward he rose, saying, "Thanks, Byron. I better get the railroad runnin' again."

"This for the *Capital Times*, Martin?" When Martin nodded, Packer said, "Mention me, will you, Martin? Say I was the inter— How do you pronounce that damn word? It means questioning."

"Deputy Byron Packer was one of the interrogators, I'll say. That all right?"

Byron smiled. "Fine, Martin. Now if you could just not mention Ritter, it would be even better."

Martin smiled. "I never intended to mention him. Thanks again, Byron."

Fourteen

From the *Capital Times*:

SCHAEFFER MURDER SUSPECT SEIZED BY U.S. MARSHAL

A reservation Indian known only as Joe was captured by two deputy U.S. marshals Monday, and is being held in the county jail of Summit County at Crater for questioning in the shotgun death of agency employee Morton Schaeffer last June. U.S. Marshal Wes Wilbarth is in Crater today, interrogating the suspect with the aid of Deputy Sheriff Byron Packer. Deputy U.S. Marshals Sam Kennery and Anson Newford are credited with capturing the Indian and removing him from the reservation to a safe jail.

While Wilbarth was unavailable for comment, it is presumed that he chose the Summit County Jail to protect the Indian from the same fate that befell Mort Schaeffer, who was killed en route to testify in the criminal fraud trial of Big Dad Herrington and Indian agent Con Brayton.

The *Times* has learned through its Primrose correspondent that Deputy Marshal Kennery was in Primrose last week and was seen in the constant company of Herrington and Brayton.

There is considerable speculation in the capital today as to the significance of this association. It is even rumored that the district attorney's office is negotiating with Brayton and Herrington before their upcoming trial, using Marshal Kennery as a go-between.

"Mother!" Tenney cried. When Mrs. Payne, startled by the anguish in Tenney's voice, turned from the stove, she saw that her daughter's face was deathly pale, her lips trembling. Tenney thrust out a newspaper to her and said, "Someone left this in the dining room. Here." She pointed to the headline and Mrs. Payne, spreading the paper, read the news story. She looked at her daughter then, and the two women stared at each other, wordless for the moment.

"Dreadful!" Mrs. Payne said softly. "That ruins Sam's plans."

"What if Sam hasn't seen this? What if he comes back with the story that he killed the Indian? Brayton and Herrington and Carnes will kill him!"

"Surely the Indian has talked, or they wouldn't have told of his capture."

"Then why was Carnes having dinner with the other two? Why hasn't he been arrested? Or why hasn't he run?"

"Yes. Why hasn't he?"

"Maybe Sheriff Morehead is watching them. Surely, if Carnes is guilty, they'll ask Morehead to arrest him," Mrs. Payne said.

"But what if Sam doesn't see this issue of the *Times*? What if none of them in Crater sees it? What if Sam is on his way back? Who knows him to tell him?"

"Did he tell you when he was coming back?"

Tenney shook her head. "He's told you everything he's told me — only that he'll take the train back. Somebody's got to get word to him, Mother."

"Morehead?"

"Won't he be needed here to arrest Carnes?"

The entrance of Mary, the other waitress, ended the conversation, but when Tenney returned to the dining room with a tray of desserts, she felt her heart still pounding wildly. She told herself that Sam was bound to know of the *Times* story. But was he? What if he had changed his plans and was riding back across the reservation, out of touch with all news of the outside world? Or if he took the train back, as he said he would, nobody would recognize him to tell him. The very fact that Brayton, Herrington, and Carnes had unconcernedly eaten their dinner in this room earlier meant that up until this very moment, Wilbarth and the others had failed to get information from the Indian. Or could it mean that the Indian had talked — implicating someone other than Carnes? She could only answer that by falling back on Sam Kennery's judgement that it was probably Carnes who had killed Schaeffer.

She distributed the desserts and refilled water glasses, almost unaware of what she was doing. Why hadn't Brayton and Herrington been arrested for paying a man, namely Sam Kennery, to kill the Indian? She thought she knew the answer to that one. Herrington and Brayton, along with Carnes, would deny the whole story and doubtless would accuse Sam of making it up to shore up the government's case against them. After all, it was one man's word against the word of three others. That must be so, or Marshal Wilbarth would have ordered Morehead to arrest Carnes. All of it, Tenney thought, added up to the fact that Sam must be told before he reached Primrose that the three men knew he had betrayed them.

On her way back to the kitchen, Tenney made up her mind. She found her mother busy scraping plates. Coming up beside her, Tenney said, "Mother, stop a minute and let me talk to you."

While Mrs. Payne was washing her hands at the big sink, Mary brought out a tray of dishes and left. Tenney moved over next to her mother then. "Mother, shouldn't I go to Junction City and head Sam off?"

Mrs. Payne gave Tenney a look of incomprehension. "How would you find him, Tenney?"

"There's only one train a day from Crater that carries passengers. If Sam had come in on that last night, he would have taken a train here this morning, wouldn't he?"

Mrs. Payne nodded and Tenney went on, "I have time to change clothes and take the train to Junction City. It gets in before the train from the north. I can wait at the depot and find out if Sam's on tonight's train. If he isn't, I'll wait for tomorrow night's train and the next night's, if I have to. If I miss him and he slips by me, I'll be at the depot, watching the train to here every morning. How can I miss him?"

"Tenney, surely he'll have heard." It was a half-hearted protest, a mother's protective urge.

"Do you read the paper every day, Mother? Do I? Then why should Sam?"

"I know," Mrs. Payne said quietly.

"I'm going, Mother. I have some time off coming. We've got enough money for the train fare. Mary's sister can take my place while I'm gone."

"Then go, Tenney. Hurry now and change clothes. I'll ask Mary about her sister."

Tenney hugged her mother and then ran across the kitchen to the door that led into their rooms.

Fifteen

Sam waited for the early morning train at Crater, watching through the depot's dirty windows a swirling snowstorm that had started around midnight. The night telegrapher sold him his ticket and Sam paced the overheated waiting room as the train was made up for the journey south. He reviewed last night's maddening, almost farcical questioning of Joe. Yesterday evening, Wilbarth had given up his plan to starve Joe of sleep. When Wilbarth ordered the windows closed and Joe covered with blankets, it was less a humanitarian move than a necessary one. Joe, shivering, was literally asleep on his feet, sustained between Packer and Anse. Joe was a heavy man, and the weight of his limp body had exhausted the two men supporting him. Wilbarth and Sam had spelled them, but it soon became apparent that Joe would exhaust them also. They made a ridiculous picture — two men dragging a snoring burden around a too-narrow cell — and Wilbarth, realizing that Joe had won, ordered him to be put on the cot and covered. Afterwards, Wilbarth, leaving Packer as the corridor guard, left the courthouse with Sam and Anse. Two days and three nights of questioning had brought not a word from Joe. He couldn't, or wouldn't, understand that Brayton had not only betrayed him, but had paid for his death. Tomorrow a court-appointed lawyer would take over for Joe.

Wilbarth and Anse would wait over another day to see Joe arraigned and indicted, but Sam had been ordered back to Primrose.

When the train pulled alongside the depot platform, Sam saw that he was the only passenger from Crater. He passed the time of day with the bundled-up brake man and then stepped into the empty passenger car. He chose a seat in the middle of the car, where drafts from both doors would be the least chilling, threw his blanket roll on the overhead rack, then slacked into the seat. He was surprised to find that these past nights, when his ration of sleep had been short and uncomfortable, sometimes nonexistent, had not tired him. Though his body was weary, his mind wasn't; the frustration of Joe's silence was riding him. He and Wilbarth had relied so heavily on Joe's eventual cooperation that they had not planned beyond that, in case Joe kept his silence. The original plan was for Sam, equipped with Joe's confession and a murder warrant for Carnes' arrest, to return to Primrose and take him into custody. Now they had no plan, or rather a half-plan that seemed unlikely of success. Sam was to return to Primrose and tell the trio that they were rid of Joe, whose body would be hidden by the winter snows that were already here in the high country, and claim his hundred dollars. He did have in his blanket roll Joe's stinking buckskin shirt, bloodied by a butcher-shop steak. If this was not proof enough, he was not to argue, but instead to good-humoredly accept their verdict on the payment. It was hoped by both Wilbarth and Sam that this would further ingratiate Sam with them, and that they would let fall information that would solidly implicate Carnes. *Pretty creaky,* Sam thought wryly.

Sam took off his jacket, rolled it up to use as a pillow, and closed his eyes. Drowsily he thought of Wilbarth's frustration too. Wilbarth was a good man, Sam reflected. The average lawman had fought Indians at one time or another, and considered them subhuman. At the hands of an officer other than Wilbarth, Joe would have been beaten within an inch of his life or tortured in the same manner that Indians had tortured white men. Wilbarth, however, had treated Joe's rights as he would have treated a white man's, even though the solution to a heartless murder lay in Joe's dark, secretive mind. Then, in spite of the rattling, jolting train, welcome sleep overtook him.

He slept fitfully most of the day, and he was still sleeping when the brakeman came through the half-filled car, its overhead lamps lighted against the outside dark, to call out, "Junction City. End of the line. Junction City."

The other passengers filed past him as the train ground to a halt. He rose, put on his jacket, lifted down his blanket roll, and then noticed that the car was swaying slightly. What Sam had thought was the natural roll and sway of the car on the trip down had been exaggerated by driving wind that was now buffeting the car. When he stepped out into the vestibule, the full force of it hit him and he knew that this was the prelude to the snowstorm they had run out of in the early afternoon. Stepping down onto the platform, Sam shouldered his blanket roll and was heading for the row of hacks when he heard a woman's voice call out from behind him, "Sam! Sam Kennery!"

Sam turned and saw Tenney running toward him. She was bundled up in a heavy ponyskin coat, and was holding onto her tiny hat as she came up to him and halted.

"Why, Tenney. What are you doing here?"

"Waiting for you. That's all. Just waiting for you, and thank the Lord you're here."

"What's happened?" Sam asked. The wind almost whipped the words out of his mouth.

Tenney said, "Let's go inside where we can talk, Sam. I've got something to show you."

Sam took her arm and they moved toward the big depot and into the high-ceiling waiting room. It was almost deserted, and was warm and quiet.

Now Sam turned Tenney to face him, his hands on her arms, and looked closely at her face. She did not look troubled; on the contrary, her eyes held a strange excitement. Her dark hair, piled on top of her head, was windblown and fetching.

"What have you go to show me, Tenney?"

For answer, she shrugged Sam's hands away and reached in her handbag and drew out a newspaper, which she unfolded. She was watching him as she did so. "Have you seen the *Capital Times*?" she asked.

Sam shook his head and Tenney gave him a strange smile that seemed to hold, beyond its sweetness, a kind of relief.

"It's on the front page, Sam. Go over by the lamp."

Halting by the lamp, Sam shook out the newspaper. Tenney had circled the story with ink, and his attention went to it immediately. As he read Macandy's story, despair washed over him, and on its heels came a wild anger. This, then, was the dead end of their plan — its aims revealed to Herrington, Brayton, and Carnes. There was bitterness in the set of his mouth as he quietly folded the paper and turned to regard Tenney. Now he understood why Tenney was here.

"You came to warn me, Tenney," Sam said simply.

She nodded. "I couldn't let you meet them again, thinking you had them fooled. They could have trapped you and killed you."

"And would have," Sam said grimly.

"What are you going to do, Sam?"

Sam shook his head. "That's too quick, Tenney." He gestured toward one of the benches. "Let's sit down."

Tenney led the way over to the nearest bench, where Sam had dumped his blanket roll, and they both sat down. Tenney had sense enough not to speak, nor could she have if she had wanted to. Sam was on his feet again immediately, and now, fists jammed in his jacket pockets, he began pacing up and down the aisle between the two rows of benches. Tenney watched his head-down, measured pacing, trying to guess what he was thinking.

Sam's thoughts, now that the first shock had worn off, were distorted with anger, and he had sense enough to know it. Where had Red Macandy gotten this story? Remembering Ben Harness in Primrose, he guessed that Red had a correspondent in Crater, but how had the correspondent gotten the story? Then he remembered that the story had said Deputy Byron Packer had aided in the interrogation, which was a lie. That was it. Packer, to gain a measure of self-importance, had spilled the story to the Crater correspondent, who would have had to telegraph it in to make today's newspaper. Then a thought came to him so abruptly that he halted. Couldn't this game of revelation by newspaper be worked two ways? It was worth trying, anyhow. He walked directly to Tenney and halted before her. "Where are you staying, Tenney?"

"Mrs. Schell's rooming house. She's a friend of mother's."

"I'll take you there," Sam said gently. "We'll see if she has room for me too."

They went out into the wind then, and Sam steered Tenney toward the hack stand where a pair of carriage lamps shone. The wind buffeted them and Tenney stopped, to catch her balance, Sam thought, before she said, "Where are we going, Sam?"

"To take a hack to the rooming house."

"But it's only three houses down Main Street from here. We can see it from here. Let's walk it."

It was useless trying to talk in the gusting night winds as Tenney, with Sam's arm in hers, guided them down the street and indicated the house. Tenney led the way into the big front parlor, where a lamp in the window was burning dimly.

"Mrs. Schell!" Tenney called.

From the back of the house came a woman's voice: "Is it you, Tenney?"

Sam heard footsteps coming down the corridor, and

then a pleasantly plump woman of forty stepped into the room.

"This is the friend I was meeting, Mrs. Schell. He's Sam Kennery. Sam, this is Mother's friend, Mrs. Schell."

Mrs. Schell gave him a swift, appraising glance. Apparently liking what she saw, she came over and extended her hand, which Sam accepted. Her black dress could have been widow's weeds, Sam guessed.

Tenney said, "Do you have a room for him tonight Mrs. Schell?"

"Down the hall from yours, Tenney. Would you like to look at it, Mr. Kennery?"

"I'll like it if Tenney does, and I'm sure she does," Sam said, and smiled.

"Then she can show you, Mr. Kennery. Those steps are getting steeper every day for me." She turned, saying, "Good night. Breakfast is at six-thirty for the early morning train."

Alone with Sam now, Tenney moved over to the sofa and sat down. "You want to talk now, Sam?"

"No," Sam said gently. "Either I'm a genius or a fool, but I've got an idea, Tenney. If it works, I'll talk as long as you'll listen. I've got to go now."

Tenney looked disappointed, but she rose. "I'll help Mrs. Schell with the morning stuff, Sam. Will you —" She halted, leaving her question unasked. "If I don't see you later, good night, Sam."

"I think you'll see me, Tenney, because I want you to. You see, you're a part of all this. You've paid for your ticket over and over, and you did again tonight."

Sam, moving toward the door, now halted halfway,

turned, and said gravely, "You're pretty, Tenney. Anybody ever tell you that?"

Tenney nodded, blushing. "Mostly people I don't want to hear it from."

"Like me?" Sam teased.

"Not like you," Tenney said.

Sam stepped out into the windy night and headed toward the business district, impatience riding him. He could see the distant lights in the capitol building on its river bluff, and recalled his last meeting with Wilbarth. Would the marshal approve of what he was about to do? Sam didn't know, and there was no time to get the authority. Besides, Wilbarth, now that they knew and respected each other, would probably tell him to use his own judgement.

Of a passerby who looked like a townsman, Sam asked directions to the *Capital Times*, and was given them. He supposed the *Times* would be closed at this hour, but he had to start his search for Red Macandy somewhere. When he rounded the corner and turned off Main Street, he saw that there was a lamp burning dimly in the *Times* building; probably the night light, he thought, but went on. Moving up to the front window, he saw a lamp burning in the rear. Rising on tip-toe to look above the painted section of the window, he could see a man wearing an ink-stained apron, fiddling with the press in the rear. Sam tried the door, found it unlocked, and walked into the big ink-smelling room. He found the swing-gate in the railing and headed back toward the gray-haired printer, who looked up at his approach. Sam halted and said, "I'm looking for Red Macandy."

"Try the saloons," the printer said curtly.

"Any special one?"

"The Prairie House or the Grandview."

Sam's glance dropped to the printer's grease-covered hands. "You got trouble?"

"You could call it that," the printer said sourly. "If I don't get this damned thing fixed by four o'clock, there'll be no *Times* tomorrow."

"What happens at four o'clock?"

"That's when I start the press run."

"Why then?" Sam asked curiously.

"To catch the early trains, is what Macandy says." He snorted. "What do those farmers and cowpunchers care if the paper's a day late? They can't read anyway."

Before Sam could thank him, the printer was attacking the press with a wrench.

On the windy street again, Sam retraced his steps to the Prairie Hotel. Its small saloon did not hold Red Macandy, and Sam wondered now if his five-second look through a keyhole at Red had been sufficient for him to recognize the newspaperman again. He thought it had been.

A block farther down Grant Street was the Grandview, and Sam headed for it. The gusty wind was driving great banners of dust down the street, and Sam, head down, bucked it to the street entrance of the Grandview saloon. Through the tall, glassed door, he could see that the saloon was doing a thriving business. Sam went in and moved slowly past several card games, glancing at each player and spectator.

Achieving the crowded bar, he took up a position

around its curve so that he could see the faces of the customers. His glance traveled down the line and stopped on one man. This had to be Red Macandy, just as Sam had last seen him, waving a thoroughly chewed cigar in the next man's face to emphasize a point.

Sam moved down the bar and bellied up to it beside Macandy. Red's hat was pushed to the back of his head, and his townsman's suit was as rumpled and dusty as if he had rolled in the street.

Sam heard him say, "You politicians are all alike. You stink."

The fat man he was addressing laughed. "Coming from a man who hasn't had a bath in two months, that's kind of funny, Red."

Sam did not miss the good-natured contempt in the fat man's tone of voice.

The bartender came up as Sam was unbuttoning his jacket.

"Your best whiskey," Sam said. As he expected, Red turned at the sound of a new voice, and Sam brushed his jacket open to put his hand in his pocket, a maneuver calculated to reveal the marshal's badge on his chest. He did not look at Red, but he knew that Red had seen the badge.

Sam put a coin on the bar, and was silent as the bartender set a labeled bottle and a glass in front of him. He was pouring his drink when Red said, "That's a marshal's badge, ain't it?"

Sam turned his head and regarded Macandy carefully. Red's drink-puffed face and bloodshot eyes showed a sham belligerence that was part of the aggressiveness he liked to show the world.

Sam said quietly, "Deputy marshal's badge."

"You a new boy for Wilbarth?"

"No."

"Well, if you're looking for him, he ain't here."

Sam said quietly, "I know. I left him in Crater this morning."

Now Red turned to face him, and Sam could see the gray sprinkling of cigar ashes on his coat front. Red was examining him carefully, and Sam poured his drink.

"Sam Kennery! Is that it?" Red said.

"That's right."

Red's next question was a pounce. "Has Joe talked yet?"

Sam looked at him coldly. "Who are you?"

"You know damned well who I am," Red snarled. "That's why you came up beside me. Has he?"

"Of course," Sam lied.

"Who was it?"

Sam looked at him wonderingly. "You must think I'm simple."

"You were the man in Wilbarth's closet, weren't you?" At Sam's nod, Red said, "Come on. Who'd Joe name?"

"You'll know when the arrest is made," Sam said.

"You going to make it?"

"Tomorrow."

"Here? Where?" Red pushed.

Sam smiled faintly and shook his head.

"Where's Wilbarth? Still at Crater?"

"I told you I left him there."

"What's he doing?"

Sam pretended to weigh the question, examining the bounds of discretion. Then he said, "There's the confession to take down, then the arraignment."

"Come on," Red wheedled. "Name the man. I won't print his name until you say so."

Sam had his drink under Red's watchful gaze. Sam set down his glass and said, "Nothing doing, Red."

"Why'd you hunt me up?" Red demanded.

"Wilbarth wanted you to know I was the man in the closet."

"So I'd get off his back? I don't believe it."

Sam only shrugged and pushed away from the bar, but Red asked quickly, "Where do you go tomorrow? You can't get out of town without I know it."

"Good night, Red," Sam said.

Outside the saloon, Sam headed directly across the street into the haven of a darkened storefront doorway. Thanks to the darkness and the blowing dust, his hiding place wouldn't be visible from across the street. Watching the doors of the saloon, he saw them open, and Red Macandy stepped out into the wind, holding his hat by its brim to keep it from being swept down the street. Red moved out to the edge of the plank walk, and peered up and then down the street, and Sam knew Red was looking for him. Afterwards, Red turned down the street and Sam, keeping behind him and on the opposite side of the street, followed him.

Red turned into the Prairie House. Sam backed into a doorway out of the wind, and waited. In less than three minutes, Red came out and again headed down the street, with Sam trailing him. When Red turned the next corner, Sam crossed the street, a sudden burst of hope within him. At the corner of the building, he looked down the cross-street and saw Red angling across the empty street toward the *Times* building. Sam waited until Red had entered it before he turned and headed back to Mrs. Schell's rooming house.

As he approached it, he saw the dimly burning lamp and felt a keen sense of disappointment. This looked like a night lamp, which meant that Tenney had given in to weariness and gone to bed. Letting himself into the house, he looked around the dim living room. There, in a big leather chair, Tenney was huddled, her knees drawn up, her skirt spread over her feet. She was sleeping.

Quietly, Sam moved across the rug to the lamp and turned it up. The added light awakened Tenney and she sat up, smiling sleepily.

Sam took off his hat and jacket and tossed them on the sofa, then swung a straight-backed chair in front of Tenney, with its back to her. He straddled the chair, folded his arms atop its back, and looked fondly at Tenney.

"Are you an idiot or are you a genius?" Tenney asked quietly.

Sam smiled. "I think a genius, Tenney, but it's too early to tell."

He told her then of his search for Red Macandy, beginning at the *Times* office. He said he hadn't found Red there but he did learn that the *Times* would not be printed until four tomorrow morning. This was a bit of blind luck, as Tenney would see later, he said. He went on to tell of hunting down Red, and a look of puzzlement came into Tenney's face.

Continuing, Sam told her of the flat-out lie he had told Red when he said that Joe had talked and identified his accomplice, who, still nameless, would be arrested tomorrow. He proceeded then to tell her of following Red to the *Times* office.

He finished by saying, "He was excited, Tenney. I think he went back to write up the story for the *Times*."

Tenney looked puzzled. "But none of what you told him is true, Sam. What does the lie get us?"

"I'm hoping it will force Carnes into running. If he does, there's the proof he's the man Joe named."

"But that isn't catching him."

"If he runs, I'll catch him, Tenney. Tomorrow morning I'll telegraph Morehead not to let Carnes out of his sight. If Red prints what I hope he does, copies of the *Times* will be on our train. I want to give Carnes time enough to read it before I hunt him up."

"It's a dangerous bluff, Sam. What if he calls it?"

"He can't afford to call it, Tenney. He can't help but think, 'What if the story is true?'"

Tenney said quietly, "He may shoot you, Sam."

"Yes. There's that," Sam agreed.

"That doesn't worry you?"

Sam grinned faintly. "Would I be in this business if it did?"

Tenney shivered involuntarily. "But it worries me," she said, almost sharply.

"I'm sort of glad it does."

Tenney looked startled. "Why on earth would you be?"

"It makes me think I'm a little bit special."

Tenney said softly, "Oh, Sam, you are. That's just it."

"You want me to give up on Carnes, Tenney?"

"No. No."

Sam unfolded his arms and put out his hands, palms up. Tenney put her small hands in his.

"Then take what comes, Tenney. Because we're both what we are, we won't change it."

Still holding her hands, he stood up and swung his leg over the chair, then drew her up and into his arms. When she looked up, expecting and wanting him to kiss her, he did. Gently, then, he moved her away from him, his hands on her forearms. "This morning I said you were pretty, Tenney. Now you're beautiful."

"I feel beautiful," Tenney said softly.

Gently, Sam turned her around and said quietly from behind her, "Go up and dream we're lucky, Tenney. Good night."

Sixteen

From the *Capital Times*:

OTHER SCHAEFFER KILLER TO BE NAMED AFTER ARREST

According to information received late last night, the Indian held in the Summit County Jail at Crater has named his accomplice in the September shotgun slaying of Morton Schaeffer. Arrest of the accomplice, whose name was not disclosed, will be made today. Place of arrest was not given. While Deputy U.S. Marshal Sam Kennery is making the arrest, Marshal Wes Wilbarth remains in Crater, seeking the arraignment on a murder charge of the Indian called Joe. No motive has been given for the accused pair's killing of Schaeffer, but it is known that Schaeffer was to be the prime government witness in the much delayed trial of Big Dad Herrington and Indian agent Con Brayton for criminal fraud.

The name of the alleged accomplice will be given to the *Times* after the arrest has been effected.

Sam, standing at a distance from Tenney, watched

her read it. When she finished, she lifted her glance and smiled. Afterwards, she took her place in the ticket line two places behind him. His own copy of the *Capital Times* was rammed in his jacket pocket; Red's story contained all he had hoped for.

Sam and Tenney had agreed at breakfast this morning that she and Sam should appear to be traveling singly and not together. This was at Sam's insistence. He did not want Tenney to appear involved in any way in this case before Brayton, Herrington, and Carnes were behind bars.

When Sam moved up to buy his ticket, he first paid for it, then thrust a folded sheet of paper in front of the ticket agent. It read: "To Sheriff Morehead, Primrose: Keep the shotgun owner in sight at all times until I see you today. See today's *Times*. Kennery."

"Will that telegram beat me to Primrose?" Sam asked.

Perry, the station agent, looked at him and said tartly, "If you didn't think so, why are you sending it?"

"Fair question," Sam said agreeably, and paid for the telegram.

Stepping out of the line now, Sam hefted his blanket roll onto his shoulder and headed for the train alongside the wet, rain-drenched platform. He had made it almost to the door when he felt someone touch his arm. He turned and saw Red Macandy standing there, his black raincoat glistening with rain.

"Where to? Primrose?" Red asked.

Sam grinned. "Well, the train stops at West Haven, New Hope, and Primrose. Take your choice."

"I can find out from Perry quick enough. You sent a telegram too. Who to?"

"Can't you find that out from Perry too? Even the message?"

"For a little money, yes," Red said bluntly.

"Then spend it," Sam said, and shouldered past him.

"Walt a minute," Red called. And again Sam halted. "You walked in here with a pretty girl. Who is she?"

"Ask her," Sam said. "We stayed at the same rooming house last night, and I walked her to the station with her umbrella."

"She bought a copy of the *Times*, read something in it, looked at you, and smiled."

"Some people look at me and *laugh*," Sam said coldly.

"You know her," Red accused.

"No, but if you do, introduce me."

"Ahhh," Red said in disgust. He reached inside his raincoat, brought out a cigar, and wedged it in the corner of his mouth. "Come on. Name me Joe's friend, Kennery. I'll get it after you arrest him today, anyway. Why not now?"

"Goodbye, Red," Sam said, pushing open the depot door. Tramping across the platform in the rain, he marveled at the gall of this man who seemingly would ask anyone, anytime, anywhere, questions whose answers were none of his business.

Sam took his seat on the train, toward the rear of the single passenger car, and minutes later he regretfully watched Tenney move down the aisle and take a seat at the front end of the car. After last night, there were a thousand things he wanted to ask her. One of them was if she would marry him. Most of what he really knew of her through their few brief meetings he had learned from her mother. They simply hadn't had time to get to know each other. Yet Sam was glad they had decided to travel separately, and the wisdom of his decision was underlined by his meeting with Red. He wanted desperately to protect Tenney and her mother until this whole affair was finished.

All through the morning, the train drove through a rain whose low clouds shrouded the distant Rafts and puddled the dusty plains into mud. The Raft River, now placid after its charge down the mountains and foothills, was pocked with raindrops and was turning from its usual green-black into the color of mud.

When the train pulled in at the Primrose depot, the rain was still holding. Sam let the car empty, and then moved outside and splashed through the rain to the protection of the depot's overhanging roof. He watched the baggage car unload under the impatient gaze of the hack drivers from the Primrose House and the Consolidated Mine. The Primrose driver received a trunk, which was hoisted onto his broad shoulders by the brakeman, and a square bundle wrapped in old newspapers, which Sam was sure was the Primrose House's ration of today's *Capital Times*.

He turned his head to see Tenney seated with a couple of the train's other passengers in the waiting hack. As the hack driver adjusted his burden, someone said, on Sam's blind side, "Hello, Mr. Kennery."

Sam turned to see Ben Harness grinning at him, looking small but cheerful in an oversized raincoat that was obviously borrowed.

"So Red's been on the telegraph," Sam said wryly.

"That's right. It looks like today's the day I earn my money."

"How you going to earn it?"

"Follow you until you make an arrest."

"Don't follow too close," Sam said quietly.

"You expecting trouble?"

"I'm always expecting trouble. You just keep out of the way."

The hack pulled out into River Street and headed for the bridge. Sam turned up the collar of his duck jacket and stepped out into the rain. Ben Harness, remembering Sam's admonition, waited until Sam reached the bridge before he followed.

Seventeen

When one of the depot loafers stopped by Sheriff Morehead's office in midmorning, the sheriff was in another county office down the corridor. The loafer, regretting the loss of the price of a couple of beers that Morehead would have given him, had he been there, nevertheless left the open telegram on the desk. When Morehead returned to his office some minutes later, he found the telegram and, without seating himself, read it. The man with the shotgun referred to Carnes, of course, but why hadn't Kennery named him? Probably today's *Times* would answer that question.

Morehead folded the telegram, put it in his shirt pocket, then walked over to the coatrack, took down his cracked yellow slicker, and put it on. His hat was still wet from his walk to work in the rain, and when he put it on, it felt cold and heavy and uncomfortable. Strange, how insignificant things were beginning to annoy him lately, he thought, and he put it down to his age, which was over fifty. The wet hat was a little thing, but were the other irritations?

As he tramped down the corridor and let himself out into the rain, he reviewed the incidents that nagged at him. Perhaps the gravest, the most hurtful, was the inescapable feeling that he was being ignored in this Herrington, Brayton, and Carnes business. It was left up to a slip of a girl to tell him that Brayton and Herrington had paid Kennery money to kill an Indian. Come to think of it, why hadn't he been asked to arrest them both for paying for a murder? And why hadn't Kennery asked him, instead of little Tenney, to check the hotel register for the date when Carnes had rented his room? That was his business, and Selby would have cooperated with him and kept his mouth shut. Was Kennery in such a confounded hurry that he couldn't write him, telling him all the things he had to learn from Tenney? He was being treated like some country Reuben who couldn't be trusted with the chores of his office. He had to learn from the *Capital Times*, and not from the marshal's office, that Kennery had captured his Indian. And what was Tenney, missing from the dining room, doing in Junction City yesterday?

Then his common sense said to him, *Quit it. You're getting older, your hip aches, and it's raining, so you're feeling sorry for yourself.* Still, this feeling of neglect nagged at him as he mounted the veranda steps of the Primrose House, peeled off his slicker, and shook it and his hat free of water before entering the lobby.

He knew Brayton and Herrington and Carnes would be in the saloon, because they always were. As a matter of fact this wasn't a bad time or a bad day to have a drink for himself. As he passed the lobby sofa to the right of the barroom door, he threw his slicker on it and then moved into the bar. As he crossed its threshold, he heard the distant sound of the morning train whistle, which, carried by the damp air, seemed closer and louder than usual.

The three polecats, as he privately called them, were seated at their regular table, with Carnes, as usual, facing all entrances, his back to a wall. That was the mark of a hardcase or a hated lawman, he thought wryly, as Alec moved up behind the bar to serve him.

Alec was pouring his drink when Herrington called out, "We're still here, Sheriff," and gave his annoying laugh.

Morehead half-turned and regarded them sourly. "You better be," he grated. As he turned back to his drink, Morehead spat in the cuspidor at his feet, a gesture of contempt he hoped would not go unnoticed. The sight of them reminded him of another grievance. If the Indian had talked, why hadn't Wilbarth telegraphed him to pick up these three owlhoots? Even if he hadn't talked, why was Wilbarth allowing them to run free? Why was he talking to a newspaperman instead of to a brother law officer? Why was Wilbarth sending Kennery down to make an arrest that he, as sheriff, could easily make? Did Wilbarth want the glory of their arrest to go to his own office?

Then, for the first time since he was a young man, he had a second morning drink, pouring it slowly and carefully.

This drink he sipped, killing time until the newspapers were brought in from the hotel hack. He had almost finished this slow second drink when, reflected in the bar mirror, he saw Tenney cross the lobby, heading for the dining room. Two strangers, both of them men, angled off toward the desk, followed by the hack driver carrying the guests' baggage, which he placed beside the desk. The driver went out again and, in a few moments, came in with the newspapers.

When Mr. Selby had finished registering the guests, he moved over to the bundle of newspapers and opened it.

Seeley Carnes, his attention attracted by the conversation, which meant the hack was in, rose now, walked past Morehead, and headed across the lobby, toward the desk. Deliberately, Morehead finished his drink, turned, and walked out into the lobby. Carnes, he saw, had finished glancing at the *Times*' first page. Lazily, he folded it, rammed it in his hip pocket, then headed across the lobby toward the stairs and, presumably, his room.

Morehead picked up a copy from the stack of newspapers on the desk, put down his money, and took a seat in a lobby chair by one of the windows. He spread out the newspaper on his crossed legs, and began to scan the columns.

The Schaeffer story caught his attention immediately. He read it hurriedly, then read it again, this time more thoroughly, and now its information fleshed out the bare bones of Kennery's telegram. Surely, Kennery was coming today to arrest Carnes, upon whom Morehead had been instructed to keep an eye. It came to him with shock, then, that Carnes had already read the story and was now up in his room. Morehead rose and moved swiftly to the veranda doors and looked down the street. Where in hell was Kennery? Why hadn't he come in the hotel hack? Had he missed the train, or changed his mind about coming?

The sense of urgency almost smothered Morehead's breathing. Carnes would be starting to run, and what was he doing about it except looking down the street for the man who would make the arrest?

He came to a sudden decision. Turning, he hurried across the lobby to the stairs and mounted them swiftly, his boots thumping as he climbed. In the second-floor corridor he turned left, remembering that ten was the number of Herrington's and Carnes' room. Drawing his gun, he approached the door. Should he knock? Hell, no. He'd surprise Carnes if he could. It was only when he was reaching for the doorknob that he realized his footfalls on the hardwood floor had announced him. Recklessly he wrenched at the doorknob, found the door unlocked, swung it open with a crash, and stepped inside. Carnes, his slicker on, his blanket roll on the bed beside him, was facing the door, his gun drawn.

Carnes fired, and Morehead felt something slam into his side, whirling him around and driving him off-balance. He shot then, even as he was falling. The next instant, he crashed down on his back, his head hitting the floor with such violence that there was an explosion of light in his eyes before black oblivion took over.

Morehead's bullet knocked Carnes' left leg from under him and turned him so that he fell on the bed, face down. As he rolled over and lunged to his feet, he could feel only a numbness in his leg, but pure panic coursed through him. The shots would draw people from below.

He stumbled for the door now, skirting Morehead's sprawled body. Once in the corridor, he heard the noise of someone charging up the stairs.

Carnes turned to the left and hobbled past Brayton's end room to the corridor window. Anchored to a hook buried in the window frame was the coiled rope of the fire escape.

Carnes smashed at the window with his gun, and in three blows, the frame was clear of glass. He took the coiled rope and flung it out the window. Holstering his gun, he threw his good leg over the sill and let himself out the window and down, dragging his hurt leg out last. The knots spaced at intervals in the fire escape rope made his descent swift and easy.

On the wet boardwalk, Carnes looked about him. A team and wagon passed down Grant Street, but its driver, huddled against the rain, had apparently neither seen nor heard his escape. Hugging the side of the hotel, he moved to the end of it. Across the muddy street, an alley's mouth gaped, and Carnes headed for it, trying not to limp and falling. His left boot was full of blood, and he knew that he would soon have to stop and tend his wound. The numbness was going, and replacing it was a searing pain in his thigh, which threatened to buckle his leg at each new step.

At the mouth of the alley, and out of sight of his escape window, he leaned against the rear wall of a building. His original plan, conceived only moments ago in his room, had been to steal a horse, any horse, that could put some distance between him and Kennery. Now he knew he could not make it to the street to steal a horse, or even commandeer one at gunpoint. Once he had it, his leg would prevent him from riding it. No, there was only one thing to do, and that was hide and stop the bleeding.

He hobbled down the alley in a mire of mud, searching both sides of the alley for a hiding place. When the hunt for him got under way, he knew these sheds he was passing would be the first to be searched. He must look for something safer, a place they wouldn't think to look.

When he was abreast of the loading dock of Pollock's Emporium, the thought came to him that a store as big as this one must have a basement. If it had a basement, there must be a loading door into it from the dock, and it would be close to the back door.

He climbed the short ladder up onto the dock, and headed for the big double doors opening into the store. He tried the latch and found the door unlocked. The door opened into a small storeroom, which held mostly kegs of nails and horseshoes, with harness and rope dangling from the wall. Beyond the big rear doors was a short corridor that led into the store itself.

This room was empty, and Carnes stepped inside, looking about him. To his immediate right he saw a pair of double doors almost as big as the one he had entered through, and he limped over to them. They had a metal latch, which he thumbed down now, swinging out one of the big doors, and peered down into blackness. But there was light enough to see a slanting ramp that vanished into the darkness. He could see that it was cleated for a foot brace to aid in the manhandling of barrel goods.

Carnes stepped inside and pulled the door closed behind him. Painfully, placing his good leg against the cleats, he lowered himself into the utter blackness.

Afterwards he stumbled into a stack of crates, and leaned against them. His leg was throbbing with every beat of his heart, but he knew a kind of relief would soon be possible.

Somewhere, surely, he thought, there must be a lantern close by, for no clerk or freighter could work in this darkness.

He pulled a match from his pocket, struck it on a crate, and looked about him. There, to one side of the ramp, was a lantern hanging on a nail. He hobbled over to it and lighted it. By its light, he moved back through a maze of barrels and crates until he came to a pile of tanned hides. He could lie down here, once he had checked his wound.

Stripping down his trousers, he saw that Morehead's bullet had entered his thigh well above the knee, and its exit had made a great tear in his flesh. Blood was still oozing from the wound. The bullet had missed the bone, he knew, or else he couldn't have walked this far. He untied his neckerchief and bound it around the wound. From his jacket pocket he took out his knife, and then, seating himself on the hides, he took hold of an edge of the top one and cut a six-inch-wide strip from it. Using the strip of soft hide as a bandage, he wound it tightly over the neckerchief and bound it by slitting the end and knotting the two halves. He waited a minute to see if the pressure of the bandage had stopped the flow of blood. Apparently it had, for there was no blood seeping out of the crude hide dressing.

He dressed himself then, shucked out of his slicker, took off his hat, and lay back on the hides. The pain was a constant, savage ache now, but it would keep him awake and alert to any surprise. Dousing the lantern, he lay back and took stock of his situation.

Joe had talked. That meant Joe would testify that Carnes had done the shotgunning of Schaeffer through the passenger coach window. It was a cinch he would hang. Herrington and Brayton couldn't help him, for they would be in jail too, for hiring Kennery to kill Joe. He'd been right all along in mistrusting Kennery, and he thought of him now with quiet hatred. If he had the sense he was born with, he would have sneaked out of Primrose the night of the day Kennery had left to hunt down Joe. Maybe he was born without any sense, he thought wryly. If proof of that were needed, why had he let Brayton send Joe along to help with Schaeffer? He knew that Big Dad wanted Brayton to be equally involved with him in Schaeffer's killing, but that was no excuse for accepting Joe as his accomplice.

He put aside these dismal thoughts and tried to concentrate on his present predicament. He couldn't hide here forever without food or water, and he would have to move out tonight, under cover of darkness. But move to where? With his leg the way it was, he couldn't ride a horse, and that meant that if he was to get out of here, it would have to be in a stolen or rented rig.

He swore bitterly and viciously. Who did he know here who would rent a rig to him? Nobody. He was the hunted, entirely surrounded by strange hunters.

Eighteen

When Sam stepped into the Primrose House lobby, he was confronted with turmoil. Tenney, still in her traveling dress, her mother, Louise Selby, and Mary were gathered at the foot of the stairs, as were a handful of townsmen. They were watching the stairs and talking excitedly among themselves.

Gray apprehension filled him then, and he walked swiftly across the lobby to Tenney.

"What's happened, Tenney?"

Tenney looked at him and he saw the backwash of fright in her face. "Morehead and Carnes had a gunfight, Sam. Morehead was hit and Carnes is gone. That's all I know."

Sam pushed through the group and took the stairs two at a time. In the upstairs corridor he could see a cluster of men around the door of Carnes' room. Even as he watched, they parted and four men carrying the sheriff's body slung in a blanket, moved out into the hall and headed toward him.

He stood aside and let them by. As they passed, he saw that sheriff's square face was ashen and his eyes were closed. The group that had parted to make way for the bearers had fallen in behind them. Kennery put out a hand and touched the sleeve of a townsman, who halted.

"Can you tell me what happened?"

"Nobody really knows. I was down in the barroom when we heard two shots. Some of us ran up here and found Morehead on the floor, shot in the side. Whoever it was that shot him kicked out that window and went down the fire escape."

Sam nodded, walked down to Carnes' room, and looked inside. There was a smear of blood on the floor by the door. Carnes' blanket roll lay on the bed. Sam wheeled and passed the closed door of Brayton's room.

Right there, he picked up the first spot of blood that somebody's bootsole had smeared on the floor. At the paneless window there was another big smear of blood, slowly being dissolved by the driving rain. It could have come from a cut made by the jagged shards of glass still remaining in the window, but Sam thought differently. No, Carnes had been shot too.

Sam looked out onto the rain-drenched street, trying to piece this together. His telegram, besides telling Morehead to watch Carnes, had told him to see today's *Times*. Had Morehead read Macandy's piece, concluded that Carnes was to be arrested, and jumped the gun by trying to make the arrest himself? That must have been the case, for Carnes had been in his room, his blanket roll readied for travel.

Where were Herrington and Brayton? They hadn't been in the downstairs crowd, or the one that had trooped after the sheriff. Had they escaped in the inevitable turmoil that followed Morehead's shooting?

Sam wheeled and headed down the corridor, and

then halted abruptly, assessing his hunch. Retracing his steps to Brayton's room, he knocked on the door. There was no answer, and he tried the doorknob and found the door locked. This made no sense, Sam thought. If Brayton and Herrington had followed their usual custom, they would have been sitting in the bar downstairs, hatless and coatless, when the shooting took place. If they'd run out into the rain, heading for the livery and horses, they would have been stopped, since everybody in town knew who they were and why they were here.

Sam came to a decision. He backed off a step from the door, drew his gun, raised his leg, and smashed his bootheel against the door, just below the knob.

The door exploded open, and Sam flattened himself against the wall next to it just as a shot boomed out from inside the room. Instantly, Sam pivoted into the doorway, crouching low, his gun raised. There by the dresser was a yellow-slickered Big Dad, his pistol tilted up as he cocked it. Sam heard the click of the hammer and saw the gun begin to descend.

He fired, and Herrington's breath was driven from him in one explosive cry as he took a step backwards, swayed, and then crashed down on his back, his gun flying out of his hand. Sam stepped back into the corridor.

"Con, throw out your gun where I can see it, and come out," Sam said flatly.

He heard a shuffling of feet on the floor inside, and then a gun arched out through the air and fell with a clatter in the doorway.

It was followed by Con Brayton, his haggard face

white with fear. He, like Herrington, was wearing a slicker and a hat.

"You and Big Dad going somewhere, Con?" Sam taunted. "Get back in there and stand away."

Brayton backed off, and Sam, after kicking Brayton's gun out into the hall, came into the room. Circling around to Herrington's head, his gun covering Brayton, he knelt and pulled open Herrington's slicker. His shot had caught Herrington high in the chest, and Sam guessed he had died within seconds. Sam rose and looked at Brayton. "He's dead, Con. You ought to envy him. You'll be dead too, but it will be a little tougher."

"You damned traitor!" Brayton exploded.

"That's right, I am," Sam agreed. "Still, I saved you a hundred dollars, Con. You can take it to the gallows with you. You're under arrest."

There came the sound of feet running in the corridor, and Sam waited for the first man to show. It turned out to be Ben Harness. The young man halted abruptly in the doorway, stared at Herrington, and then raised his glance to Sam. He saw the pointed gun and shifted his eyes to Brayton, then back to Sam.

"Is he dead?"

Sam dipped his head in affirmation. Now other men moved up behind Harness. Sam knew none of them. He would need help, and Ben Harness seemed the only one who could give him any.

"Ben, I'm stuck for help. Can you give me some?"

"I'll sure try," Ben said.

"I'm taking Brayton over to the jail. Carnes is loose on the town, if he hasn't already ridden out. Can you go to the livery and tell them Carnes might make a try for one of their horses? After that, will you hunt up the coroner to come up here for Herrington? Afterwards, come over to Morehead's office."

The young man nodded, turned, and pushed through the group of watchers.

"All right, Con. Head for the lobby."

Brayton moved to the door, and Sam, holstering his gun, fell in behind him. After closing the door on the curious watchers, Sam crossed the corridor, retrieved Brayton's gun, and rammed it in his waistband.

The lobby held even more people now, and Sam, seeing Tenney, said to Brayton, "Stop right here, Con."

Brayton halted, and Sam moved the few feet to Tenney, who was standing beside her mother.

"Where'd they take Morehead, Tenney?"

"To Dr. Price's house. His spare room is the hospital." She hesitated. "Sam what was the shooting?"

"Herrington at me, and me at him. He's dead. I'm taking Brayton over to the jail. Can you come along with me, Tenney?" He looked at her mother. "I'm still asking for help, Mrs. Payne."

"Go along, Tenney," Mrs. Payne said.

Tenney went over to get her coat from the row of hooks by the dining room door, and then she joined Sam. When she was beside him, Sam said, "All right, Con."

As the three of them moved through the crowd toward the veranda, Sam spotted the middle-aged hack driver among the watchers, and beckoned him over. "Is your team still harnessed?" he asked him.

The driver nodded. "Out front."

"Can you take us to the courthouse?"

The driver nodded and led the way out to the veranda and down the steps.

"You sit with the driver Con," Sam said.

Wordlessly, Brayton climbed up into the front seat, directly behind the horses who were glistening wetly in the still-falling rain. Sam and Tenney climbed into the rear seat, and the hack moved away from the crowd who had trailed them to the veranda.

At the courthouse, they went directly to Morehead's office. Sam, acting on a hunch that Morehead would have the jail key handy, found it hanging on a nail behind the door. When he had locked Brayton in one of the basement cells, he returned to Tenney, who in his absence, had seated herself in the straight chair behind the desk. Taking off his hat, Sam tossed Brayton's gun on the desk, then slumped into Morehead's swivel chair.

"Tenney, tell me what happened."

"Mr. Selby said Carnes was the first to buy a paper. He read the front page right at the desk. Then he put it in his pocket and went upstairs. Only seconds later, the sheriff bought a paper, sat in one of the lobby chairs, and read it. Then he moved over to the door and looked down the street — maybe for you. Then he went upstairs and then we heard the shots." She paused. "Carnes is gone, isn't he?"

Sam nodded. "I think he's shot, Tenney. I don't know how badly. He was strong enough to slide down that rope and disappear."

"You think he's still in town?"

Sam sighed. "I don't know, Tenney, and I won't, unless somebody comes here and says they saw him ride out. Until then, we can assume he's here in Primrose."

"How do we find him?"

"That's why I asked you to come along, Tenney. Did Morehead have any deputies?"

"Two, of a sort. They patrol the River Street saloons and stop the miners' fights. They're really just hired toughs."

"Then who's sheriff, Tenney?"

"Why can't you be?"

Sam shook his head. "Not without the county commissioners deputizing me. Who are the commissioners?"

"Mr. Pollock, at the store, is one. Hargreave is a rancher down south. Kimbrough is a rancher too, but he lives in West Haven."

Sam heard footsteps in the corridor, and turned his head just as Ben Harness, his black slicker streaming water, stepped into the room. At the sight of Tenney, he smiled and said, "Why, hello, Tenney. Are you under arrest?"

Sam answered for her. "Not yet," he said dryly. "Find the coroner, Ben?"

"That's Doc Price. He'll take care of it as soon as he's finished with Morehead. He took the bullet out of him, but he's mighty sick, Doc says."

"Is he conscious?"

"No, Doc said."

Sam rose, walked over to the window, and looked

199

out on the gray noonday. Then he turned and said to Ben, "Tenney tells me your boss is a county commissioner, Ben."

"Yes, sir. He's chairman."

"Does he know what sort of a problem he's got?"

"I wouldn't know, Kennery. He gave me the morning off to follow you."

Sam said grimly, "This town has to be searched for Carnes, Ben. Who leads the search? What men will do the searching? Can you and Tenney make up a list of responsible men who don't mind getting shot at?"

Harness looked at Tenney. "I think we could, couldn't we, Tenney?"

"They should all be men who'll recognize Carnes. That's where you come in, Tenney. They'll be men who ate at the hotel and drank at the bar there. While you and Ben make up the list, I'll go to the livery and pick up my horse."

As Sam went down the courthouse steps, he noted that the rain was slacking off just a little, and he considered the events of the last hour. Red Macandy's *Times* story had worked all too well, he thought. It had forced Carnes to make his move, but it could cost Morehead his life. He wished bitterly that his telegram to Morehead had contained the admonition to leave Carnes' arrest to the marshal's office. It had not occurred to him that this would be necessary, since Morehead knew the marshal's office was handling Carnes' case, just as it was handling the Brayton and Herrington case. So now they had a hunted killer to catch, and Sam had no delusions that it would be easy. Carnes wouldn't balk at killing anyone who tried to capture him, since he believed he would be tried for murder in any event.

At the livery stable, Sam picked up the horse he had rented his first day in town. He inquired of the hostler whether Carnes was boarding a horse here, and the horse was pointed out to him. Kennery asked the hostler to bring the horse into the stable, where he could be guarded, and then he rode back to the courthouse. Leaving his horse in the open-faced shed behind the courthouse, alongside Morehead's gelding, he tramped across the muddy yard and entered the side door of the courthouse.

Tenney and Ben Harness had come up with the names of a dozen men, none of whom Sam knew. He pocketed the list, saying, "Let's go see your boss, Ben."

They walked back to Main Street together, and parted from Tenney at the Primrose House corner. At Pollock's Emporium, Ben took over, leading the way back to the stairs that ascended to a balcony overlooking the store.

Pollock, in shirtsleeves, had seen them coming, and was standing when they reached his big flattop desk. He was a small man with a thin, scholarly face, and under a thatch of white hair he wore heavy, iron-rimmed glasses, which were now pushed up on his forehead.

Ben introduced them to each other, and a look of relief came into Pollock's face. He gestured toward a straight-backed chair, and Sam waited until Pollock sat down before he slacked into the chair.

"That was a tragic business with Morehead, Kennery. I understand he may not live."

"I'm sorry to hear that," Sam said. "Still, his office goes on, Mr. Pollock, and at the moment it's empty."

Pollock nodded and said almost reluctantly, "He had a couple of deputies, but both of them together couldn't do the sheriff's job."

"Would you consider deputizing me?" Sam asked. "I think Carnes is hiding here in Primrose, and there'll have to be a search for him."

He explained the necessity for someone to lead the search, and he showed Pollock the list that Ben and Tenney had drawn up of men who would recognize Carnes.

The rest was routine. Pollock swore him in and even gave him his own deputy's badge, which, along with his Bible, was stored in a desk drawer of his desk. It was agreed that Ben, during the noon hour, would get in touch with six men on the list, giving each of them another's name to speak to. After the noon meal, all of them, well-armed, would meet in the empty second-story courtroom in the courthouse. There the search plan would be discussed and warrants distributed.

Nineteen

In the darkness of the Pollock's Emporium cellar, Seeley Carnes lay listening and thinking. An hour had gone by since he had shot Morehead, and still no hue and cry had been raised for him. He had heard, dimly, two gunshots, but it was senseless trying to read any meaning into them. Why hadn't Kennery started a search for him? Did he think he had succeeded in leaving town?

He felt a fierce longing for somebody to talk with, someone who could see what was going on, who could warn him of danger. In less than an hour's time, this dark cellar had turned from a haven of safety into a torture chamber. He would have to get out of here, he knew — and quickly — but where would he go? He thought of the sporting houses, and rejected the thought of hiding in one of them. Any of those girls would turn him over to the law simply as a way of currying favor. What about the backrooms of the River Street saloons? They too would be risky, he reflected. All bartenders would be warned to be on the lookout for him. Then what about the boardinghouses and rooming houses that catered to the miners? That was a possibility, he knew, but he had heard that most of them were run by women, and women talked. What he needed was a place where he could be anonymous, where he could bribe somebody to get him food and provide him with shelter until his leg healed enough that he could ride.

He had a feeling that on the other side of River Street someone could or would hide him. In the nights of drinking with Brayton and Herrington in the sporting houses and the River Street saloons, he had learned that Primrose was two distinct communities. On the other side of the river were the miners — Germans, Irish, Canadians, Austrians, Cousin Jacks, and Italians. They were the miners, muckers, and timbermen of the Consolidated and other mines. They lived in their own rough world, which had no connection or contact with the world of ranching, horse-trading, and business that lay on this side of the river. If he could make it to River Street, he could be absorbed among that incurious, foreign, work-drugged, and drunk-sodden world of miners.

But would Kennery ever let him make it as far as River Street? Carnes thought of Kennery now with an objective hatred. Looking back on it all, he was certain that Kennery's getting the drop on Morehead at the Primrose House had been as rehearsed as any theater play. Brayton was a fool, but Big Dad had a head, if he bothered to use it. The trouble was, Big Dad had a weakness for the bad boys, and Kennery had shrewdly played on it. Kennery had trapped them into admitting they were responsible for Schaeffer's death, and only his own stubborn insistence that he not be named as Joe's accomplice had saved him till now. In fact, Kennery had pretty much had his own way, but that was only temporary. If he could make River Street and let his leg heal, then he would become the hunter, not the hunted.

It's time to move, Carnes thought. He reached out for the cold, unlit lantern. Grasping its bail, he struggled to his feet. He lit the lantern and took a few tentative steps, testing his leg. It hurt to put his weight on it, but he could walk. What if he did limp? Who knew he'd been hit? So who would suspect his limp?

Now Carnes, walking slowly, began to range the basement, sizing up what was stored here. It seemed to him that this storeroom held all the hard goods on one side — stoves, tubs, crocks, axes, pitchforks, and the like. The other side held both men's and women's clothes, shoes, boots, coats, and hats.

It was the latter side that Carnes prowled now. In minutes he had shucked off his cowman's boots, bloody trousers, and Stetson, trading them for corduroy trousers, thick-soled boots, a miner's round black hat, a red bandanna neckerchief, and a heavy wool mackinaw with pockets big enough to hold his gun on the right side and his rolled-up ammunition belt on the left. He made sure he had transferred his tobacco pouch and cigarette papers. His own clothes he rolled in a bundle, which he hid in a half-empty barrel of children's shoes. On his way from the hardware side to the ramp, he picked up a round dinner pail of the sort that every miner carried on shift. Pausing by one of the bigger crates that was covered with a quarter of an inch of dust, he rubbed his hands in the dust and then smeared his face with it.

Then he blew out the lantern and labored up the ramp.

At the top, he listened with his ear to the door. At

least two men were in the storeroom, for he heard a pair of voices in a discussion he couldn't hear clearly enough to understand. Presently, he picked up footsteps and then lost them as they receded. Lifting the latch, he opened the door onto the now-empty storeroom. Unconcernedly, he stepped out into the room, closed the door, and moved toward the rear door. It was still unlocked, and he stepped out onto the loading platform, closing the door behind him.

The rain still held, and Carnes turned up the collar of his mackinaw and, dinner pail in hand, descended the ladder and started slowly down the alley, heading toward River Street. To anyone observing him, he appeared to be only another lanky, dirty miner with muddy boots, carrying his dinner pail. When he exited from the alley, he turned toward Grant Street, heading slowly for the river. His hobbling gait attracted little attention as he moved down Grant Street. Half of the miners on the street had been crippled in mine accidents, and the townspeople were so used to their disabilities that they attracted no attention.

It was a slow journey, but Carnes reached the bridge without being intercepted, and even paused on the bridge, staring down at the rushing torrent below, while his throbbing leg was resting.

On River Street he went into the nearest saloon, ordered whiskey, and asked of an off-shift miner where a man could live here.

"The big tent. The cheapest. Out by the Consolidated dumps, it is," the man answered.

Carnes made his way past the Miner's Rest saloon and turned toward the towering dumps of the Consolidated Mine. Across a couple of vacant lots, Carnes could see the huge gray dormitory tent, sagging in the rain. This Carnes had already heard about and had forgotten, but he remembered seeing its big kerosene flare at night. It had been described to him as a place where the rootless, drifting miners could sleep off a drunk in the stinking, lice-ridden blankets of a cot. It was a place for the sick, the almost broke, the out-of-work, and the homeless. It was, Carnes thought, exactly what he wanted.

There were two horses standing out of the rain under a canvas fly over the entrance flap. Before Carnes was halfway across the road, two men came out and mounted. They were wearing yellow slickers against the rain, and one of them Carnes recognized, even at that distance, as a man who was a regular patron of the Primrose House dining room. The pair mounted and headed for the big main gates of the Consolidated.

Inside the tent, immediately to the right of the door, a surly old man took Carnes' quarter, and Carnes limped into the dim interior of the tent. There could have been a hundred cots in the tent, less than half of them occupied by off-shift miners. The stench of sweaty, dirty clothes and blankets was so overpowering that Carnes breathed through his mouth. Moving down the aisle, he took a cot as far from the door as possible, and lay down on it. It wasn't exactly elegant, he thought grimly, but it would serve until he could hunt down Kennery.

Twenty

The afternoon's search had been a thorough one, but there was just too much ground to cover and there were too many people to look at. Besides, when the day shift at the mines made way for the night shift, there would be a thousand new faces to scan. The building search had been tedious and time-consuming. By darkness, all of the wet and discouraged deputies had reported to Sam and Ben Harness at Morehead's office. To a man, they stated that there were too many places and too many shifting people to make the search effective. They were going to try tomorrow, but with a whole night before him, Carnes could either flee Primrose or hide himself in any building already searched. When the last deputy had left, Ben Harness looked at his list. "Counting me, that's the lot of them, Kennery."

From the straight chair by the desk, he watched Kennery slowly cruise the office, head down, arms folded across his chest. Presently, Ben said, "Can I go now, Kennery? I've got this story to telegraph Red tonight, and it'll be a long one."

"Sure, sure, go on," Kennery said "And thanks, Ben, for all you've done."

Ben Harness said good night and left. Sam continued his pacing. He had hoped, but hadn't really believed, that a search started only an hour after Carnes' escape would turn up his man, but the run of luck had been against him. What was there left to do now? Carnes had successfully made it to nightfall, and depending on how badly he'd been hurt, he was sure to put many miles between himself and Primrose before tomorrow's dawn. However circumspectly, he would be heading for Texas and freedom. Once there, no Texas sheriff would bother to hunt down Carnes, a Texan who had killed a Northern sheriff in a fair fight.

I've really ripped it, Sam thought bitterly. Wilbarth would be angry at his failure to corner Carnes, his failure to ward off Morehead's attempted arrest of him, his presumption in planting a lie with Red Macandy, and his failure to capture Carnes after his escape. Maybe this was the time to turn in his badge and get back to the ranch that was waiting for him.

But the idea of quitting in the face of defeat was intolerable to him. And what about Tenney? She had been an intimate witness to his failure. Although she would never call it by that name, it was what she would think.

These gray thoughts were interrupted by the sound of footfalls in the corridor. When they passed the neighboring office, Sam halted and looked at the door, wondering who was calling at this hour. A tall middle-aged man in a black rubber raincoat entered the room, and Sam noticed that underneath the unbuttoned coat, the man was wearing a townsman's suit. He was a lean man with a quietly vindictive face. Halting just inside the door, he looked stonily at Sam and said, "You have a client of mine locked up. This is the fifth time

I've called on this office this afternoon and found it locked."

"That's right. I was hunting another of your clients."

"What are the charges against Con Brayton?"

"Brand new ones, Mr. . . . Phelan, is it?"

"Thurston," the man said coldly.

"The charges are complicity in murder and complicity in attempted murder. Two counts, Mr. Thurston."

Thurston's eyebrows rose. "You can't mean it. Whose murder?"

"Morton Schaeffer's murder and paying for the murder of an Indian called Joe Potatoes. You can see your client, Mr. Thurston. The judge will have to decide if you can free him by bond."

Thurston thought this over for a long moment, and then he said dryly, "Come to think of it, I don't believe I have a client locked up. Fraud is one thing, but murder is another." He paused, "What happened between you and Herrington today, Kennery?"

"He shot at me. I shot back. He missed. I didn't. It's about that simple," Sam said. He waited a moment, then added, "You want to see Brayton?"

"Not ever," Thurston said flatly. "If he asks for me, don't bother to send for me. Good night, Mr. Kennery."

Thurston turned and walked out. Watching him go, Kennery felt a faint stirring of satisfaction, the first he had felt today. With Herrington dead and Carnes escaped, Brayton had to face the music all alone.

Well, the law would have to keep Brayton alive, and

that meant that Sam had better get the agent some supper before he got supper for himself. First, though, he should inform Wilbarth of the day's events before the marshal read of them in tomorrow morning's *Times.*

Outside, the rain had slacked off and the weather was turning colder. In the darkness of the shed, Sam cinched up the saddle of his livery horse, then sought Grant Street and the depot, wondering if the agent would still be on duty.

Approaching the depot, he saw that a lamp was lighted in the agent's office, and as he passed the window, heading for the tie rail, he saw the agent hunched over his telegraph.

Inside, Kennery picked up a telegraph blank and composed his message to Wilbarth. In a few words he wrote of Morehead's attempted arrest of Carnes, of Morehead's being shot, and of Carnes' probable wounding and escape. He stated that a search for Carnes had been unsuccessful so far, that Herrington had been killed, and that Brayton was being held in jail pending orders from the marshal. He mentioned that he had been deputized by the county commissioner and was temporarily acting as sheriff. Finally, he was awaiting Wilbarth's orders. As he turned the telegram over to the agent, he reflected bitterly on how few words it had taken to relay this mass of bad news.

Of the harried agent he requested directions to the home of Dr. Price, and was given them.

At a big frame house in the residential district a couple of blocks east of Grant Street, his knock on the door was answered by Mrs. Price. The doctor was out on a call, but had left orders that under no conditions were visitors allowed to see Morehead. Yes, he was alive, but had lost much blood and was delirious.

A few minutes later, Sam dismounted in front of a Grant Street cafe, went inside, and ordered two steaks, one of which he would eat himself. The other he would take out. The dining room at the Primrose House, where he would rather have eaten, would be closed at this hour, he knew.

Back in the courthouse, with a plate of food wrapped in a clean dish towel, Kennery got the cell key from his office and took the stairs opposite it to the basement jail. Brayton had been pacing his cell, but when Sam appeared, he came to the door.

Sam put the food on the floor and said curtly, "Back off, Brayton."

The agent did so, and Sam opened the cell door, set the plate inside, and relocked the cell.

"Is there any whiskey in there?" Brayton asked hoarsely.

"Just food," Sam replied.

"You couldn't find me a drink, could you? I'm a sick man, Kennery."

He looked a sick man, Sam thought, and for a brief moment he pondered Brayton's request. Whiskey wouldn't do him any harm, and it just might make him cooperate.

"I'll look, Con. Maybe Morehead had some in his office."

Upstairs in the sheriff's office, Kennery began his search at the desk. Sure enough, in the lower right-hand drawer was a half-full quart bottle of whiskey.

Downstairs again, Sam turned up the wick of the corridor wall lamp, then let himself into Brayton's cell and handed him the whiskey. The food he had brought was still where he had put it. When he extended the bottle to Brayton, the agent, his yellow-toothed smile trembling in anticipation, took the bottle with both hands.

Sam seated himself on the cot opposite Brayton's and watched the agent, still standing, wrench the cork from the bottle, tilt it up to his mouth, and take three gulps of whiskey so huge they would have staggered an ordinary man. The sigh that came from Brayton then was one of pure bliss, and Sam wondered how long it had been since Brayton had had six whole waking hours without a drink.

Now Brayton sat down on his cot, cradling the bottle between his knees, and regarded Sam. "You're a good lad, even if you are a traitorous bastard," Brayton said.

Sam dipped his head toward the food. "That'll get cold. Better eat it."

"Let it get cold," Brayton said scornfully. He patted the bottle. "This has got enough heat in it for me,"

Sam watched him as he took another long drink, and observed that some color had crept into Brayton's sallow, ravaged face.

Brayton said, almost reflectively, "So Joe talked."

Since it was a statement rather than a question, and didn't require an answer, Sam said only, "Kind of changes things for you, doesn't it, Con?"

A sly expression crept onto Brayton's face. "Oh no you don't, Sam. I won't talk to anybody about this unless my lawyer's with me."

"Would that be Thurston?" Sam asked innocently.

"Him or Phelan."

"Thurston came in for permission to see you. When I told him you'd be charged for complicity in murder, he said he didn't mind defending you for fraud, but murder was another thing. He doesn't want to see you and won't come if you send for him."

Brayton smiled cynically. "You're lying, Sam. Again. For about the thousandth time."

"I don't have to lie to you anymore, Con. I've got you where I want you. Herrington's dead. Carnes will make a trade with us for a life sentence instead of a hanging."

"You haven't got him."

"No. But when we catch him, he'll trade."

"What will he trade you to beat the hanging?" Brayton asked skeptically.

"He'll testify that you and Herrington paid him to kill Schaeffer. Joe will testify that you paid him too."

Brayton smiled sardonically. "What are you trying to get out of me, Sam? A signed confession?"

"I hadn't thought about it, but now that you mention it, a confession would help us both."

"How would it help me?" Brayton challenged.

Sam leaned back against the wall, raised a leg, and clasped his fingers around his knee. "Well, look at it this way, Con. You're due for a jury trial. There isn't a man in the state who hasn't read or heard about your indictment for fraud. Even if every prospective juror swears he won't be influenced by your indictment, you know and I know that just isn't true. You know what it's like? It's like a lawyer saying something before a jury that the judge orders struck from the record. He orders the jury to ignore what they just heard. Do you really think it's possible for a man to wipe words that he's just heard from his memory?"

"No," Brayton said. "That bit of court business always seemed crazy to me."

"All right. Let's go back to you, Con. You'll walk into court with that skunk in your pocket — your indictment for fraud. Carnes' testimony, Joe's testimony, and my testimony won't be pretty, Con. The jurors will already think you're a crook. Then, when you're proven an accessory to a murder and when it's proven you tried to buy a second murder, you won't have anyplace to hide from that jury. You'll wish you'd never been born, you'll wish you were dead."

Brayton, who had been watching Sam intently, now let his glance slide away. "You think a signed confession will prevent all that?"

"Hell, I'm not a lawyer and I'm not a mind-reader, Con," Sam said irritably. "I only know if you signed a confession and threw yourself on the mercy of the court, there wouldn't be a jury trial. It would be up to the judge to sentence you."

"One fool instead of twelve, is that it?" Brayton said sourly.

"Let's say a better educated fool than the other twelve."

Brayton thought about that a moment, and then lifted the bottle and drank from it. He wiped his mouth on his sleeve and then grinned crookedly at Sam. Rather than a smile of confidence, it was a sorry effort to hide despair, Sam thought.

"Oh no, Sam," Brayton said. "I'm not worried about a thing. Big Dad is dead and Carnes is loose. Joe has already told you Carnes killed Schaeffer. I'll prove that Carnes was Herrington's man and the killing was Herrington's idea. I only loaned Joe to Herrington so he could point out Schaeffer for Carnes. That makes my part in all of it mighty small."

"What about paying me to kill Joe?" Sam asked.

The agent's reply was bland. "Why, Sam, I did no such thing. It would take Carnes' and Big Dad's word to hang that on me. Like I said, Big Dad's gone to the Other Shore, and Carnes is gone like smoke. No, I didn't pay you to kill Joe, and you can't prove I did."

Sam shrugged and said indifferently, "Well, we're going to find out if I can, that's for damn sure." He rose from the cot now, and made a loose gesture in Brayton's direction. "Drink it up, Con, or leave it, but either way, give me the bottle."

"Can't I keep it for after I eat?" Brayton protested.

"No. If I left it with you, you could get to thinking about what's going to happen to you. You could break it, cut your wrists, and bleed to death before I found you." He smiled faintly. "Of course, that would save us trying you, but it wouldn't look good, would it?"

Brayton glared at him with quiet hatred. The bottle was only a swallow from being empty and Brayton tilted it up and drained it.

After accepting the bottle from Brayton, Sam let himself out, relocked the cell, and went upstairs. He was thinking, as he shut the stairway doors and crossed the corridor, that he would probably have to sleep tonight on the sofa in the sheriff's office. Possibly, just possibly, Carnes might still be hanging around town. It would be like him to try and break Brayton out.

He stepped into the sheriff's office and immediately saw Tenney sitting on the straight chair beside the desk, her coat still on. He halted, and for a moment they looked at each other. Then Tenney rose, came to him, stood on tiptoe, and kissed him.

"That was for what?" Sam asked gently.

"That was because I like to do it," Tenney said. "Come sit down and tell me about today." She led him back to the desk, removed her coat, and sat down again while Sam seated himself in the swivel chair by the desk.

"Well, the best part of my day happened ten seconds ago," he said, and proceeded to recount the events of the last few hours. All through his flat-toned monologue, Tenney could see the discouragement in him. He finished by saying, "The plain hell of it is, Tenney, Brayton might walk away from Primrose a free man. If Joe Potatoes keeps his mouth shut, where are we? Joe can claim, and likely will, that he only pointed Schaeffer out to Carnes. That's a provable lie because Carnes already knew Schaeffer from having delivered beef to the agency, but Joe will stick to that story and maybe spend a short time in prison. If Brayton gets to him and promises him money and whiskey for not involving him in the Schaeffer killing, then where are we? Herrington's dead and Carnes is gone. So who do we bargain with for evidence that will convict Brayton?"

He ran a hand through his hair in a gesture that Tenney interpreted as quiet despair, and his eyes were somber as he said, "I made a mess of it, Tenney. I messed up the whole damn business."

Twenty-One

Seeley Carnes was awakened early by miners rising for the day shift mingling with men just off the night shift. Miners from the latter were in no hurry to climb into their blankets, since this was the end of their working day and the time for relaxation.

Carnes, fully dressed, threw off his blankets and, to test his leg, mingled with the men roving the aisle. His wound was achingly sore to the touch, but surprisingly, it took his weight and he knew he could walk.

Back at his cot, he sat down and considered the day that lay ahead of him. If would be foolhardy to leave the tent and risk being recognized. The search for him had probably ended, for Kennery would have reckoned that he had managed to get a horse during the night and was headed out of the state. Still, he couldn't be sure. Then there was the problem of food and drink.

Carnes looked about him in the dimly lit tent and spotted a face that looked honest and spoke to the man. He was answered in German. The second honest face belonged to a middle-aged, bent-backed Irishman who had the cot across the aisle from him. Carnes rose and hobbled over to him. The man was changing into dry boots, which indicated that he was going out.

"My friend," Carnes began, "how would you like to earn a pint of whiskey?"

The Irishman looked up at him and said pleasantly,

"That's why I've been workin' all night, lad. I would like to earn another, though. What is it you want?"

"I hurt my leg and I'd like to rest it. Could you go to one of the saloons and get me a sandwich and a pail of beer? Buy yourself a pint of whiskey and me one too, and bring them back here."

"I can do all that, but let us see your money first."

Carnes went back to the cot, took out the lunch pail from under it, came back, and set it on the Irishman's cot. Then he reached in his pocket and drew out an eagle. There was a chance, of course, that as soon as the Irishman left the tent, he would throw the bucket off in the weeds and proceed to get roaring drunk on Carnes' money, but Carnes had to take that chance. The Irishman finished tying his boots, rose, gave Carnes a grin, and walked out.

Carnes lay back on the cot. Once the food and drink problem was settled, there was some thinking to be done about the matter of cornering Kennery. The wise thing to do, of course, would be to forget Kennery, wait until night, steal a horse, and clear out of the country. Well, he could leave the country and head back to Chain Link, but not before he had evened the score with that traitor of a deputy marshal. It had taken him a good three days to recover from that beating Kennery had given him — three days during which Big Dad and Brayton, while sympathizing with him, were also laughing at him. But he'd been right about Kennery all along. The story of the beating would get back to Texas, of course, but he'd see to it that the story would end with a statement that Seeley Carnes had killed the man who beat him up. Nobody would ever be able to accuse him of accepting a beating without retaliating. When you came down to it, Carnes thought, a man wasn't even half a man if he had no pride.

If Joe Potatoes had talked, that meant that Big Dad and Brayton had been arrested and were very likely in the jail across the river right now. He wondered if his shot had killed Morehead. If it had, who was sheriff now? Kennery, of course, would stay close to Big Dad and Con, at least for a few days. With the sheriff dead or badly hurt, the prisoners would be Kennery's responsibility. Would he take them to Junction City? It really didn't matter, Carnes thought. Wherever Kennery was — Junction City, Primrose, or somewhere else — he would find him and kill him.

The Irishman came back sooner than Carnes could have hoped for. He had a free drink with Carnes out of his bottle, then left Carnes to his beer, sandwich, whiskey, and foul cigarettes.

As Carnes munched on his sandwich, he thought of all the questions he was unable to answer. He couldn't send somebody like the Irishman across the river to find out what had happened to Brayton and Herrington without risking betrayal. Somehow, in the long day that lay ahead of him, he would think of some way of learning what the situation was across the river.

Twenty-Two

When Kennery heard the knock on the door, he awoke, and for the briefest part of a second he did not know where he was. Then, when the knock was repeated, he called, "Coming," and threw the blanket off him. The sofa at the sheriff's office had made such an excellent bed that his sleep had been deep and dreamless.

Crossing to the door in his stocking feet, he opened it and found a twelve-year-old boy standing in the corridor, extending a paper to him. When Sam saw that it was a telegram, he reached in his pocket for a coin for the boy, then closed the door and moved over to the window, which gave a view of a gray, chill, though rainless day. Unfolding the telegram, he read its brief message:

Meet me at Primrose depot this morning. Wilbarth.

Moving over to the sofa, Sam folded his blanket, then sat down and began pulling on his boots. *Well, it had to come sooner or later,* he thought. Wilbarth was coming to Primrose to salvage what he could of the mess Sam had mostly created. There probably could be no criminal action against Brayton if Joe Potatoes had kept his silence. There would be no action on the criminal fraud indictment, either, since Herrington and Carnes — one dead, the other vanished — had put Schaeffer out of the way, leaving no proof that Brayton had a part in killing him. All he himself had contributed, Sam thought wryly, was the useless death of Herrington and the inexcusable escape of Carnes. Rising now, he concluded sourly that this would be one of the less pleasant days in his life.

Putting on his jacket and hat, he stepped out into the corridor and locked the door behind him. Last night, before sleep overtook him, he had realized that the presence of Brayton downstairs in the jail was a nuisance and a hindrance to any free movement on his part, and he aimed to correct that situation right now.

He found Commissioner Pollock in his store, which he had just opened and which was empty. Pollock was heading for his balcony office, his coat still on, when Sam hailed him. There in the aisle, they both decided that Sam must have a deputy. Pollock knew a man who would be willing to sleep in the sheriff's office, a guard at Consolidated Mining & Milling. Sam gave the key to the sheriff's office to Pollock, who in turn would give it to the guard, whose first duty would be to rustle up food for the prisoner.

Afterwards, Sam went up the street, turned in at the Primrose House, and went into the dining room for breakfast. Tenney, her tray loaded with other breakfasts, saw him and detoured past his table to wish him a soft and warm good morning before she went on to her other customers.

When she returned a minute later, Sam drew out

Wilbarth's telegram and handed it to her. She read it and looked at Sam with a question in her dark eyes. "Trouble, Sam?"

"What else could it be?"

"Breakfast will help," Tenney said. "The same?" At Sam's nod, she left.

A very practical woman, Sam thought fondly. *Feed the beast first and then comfort him.* Well, that had worked for women all through history, so why wouldn't it work this morning with him?

Tenney brought his breakfast and had to hurry away to wait on other customers. Sam ate Mrs. Payne's eggs, steak, and potatoes with wolfish hunger. Yesterday, he remembered, he had mostly forgotten to eat.

He was reviewing what he should do this morning before Wilbarth's train arrived, when Tenney returned to fill his coffee cup.

"Tenney, could you do something for me this morning while you're upstairs making the beds?" At Tenney's nod, he continued, "Check with Mr. Selby first to see if it's all right. If he says yes, will you move me into Con Brayton's room?"

"It's not as nice, Sam. Yours is a front room and his is a back one." She frowned. "What's behind it, Sam?"

Sam grimaced. "I've missed too many chances, Tenney, and I don't want to miss another. If Carnes is hurt and here in town, or if he's not hurt and has ridden out, the chances are he'll try and get in touch with Brayton. Maybe he hasn't heard that Herrington is dead and Brayton's in jail. He just might want to send some word to them. I want to be in Brayton's room if that message comes."

"That makes sense," Tenney conceded.

"Tell Mr. Selby not to change my number or Brayton's number in the register. Just leave everything as it is, only move me into Brayton's room."

Tenney nodded and started for the kitchen, then halted and looked searchingly at Sam. "Nothing's your fault, Sam. Just keep believing that."

Kennery smiled crookedly. "I wish that would fix things, but it won't, Tenney."

He finished his coffee, left the Primrose House, and headed up the street to the livery, where he checked to see if anyone had come in late in the day or after dark yesterday to rent a horse or a rig. Receiving a negative answer, he headed for Dr. Price's house. There he was told by Mrs. Price that Morehead's condition had worsened and that the doctor, who had been called over to the scene of a mine accident, thought it was touch and go with the sheriff. Then Sam tramped back through the chill morning to the courthouse.

He found Matt Fisher, the Consolidated guard, waiting for him. Fisher was a big young man who looked as if he could handle himself. He had already fed Brayton, and Sam told him to return the dishes to the cafe, and that he would be here until train time.

After Fisher went out on his errand, Sam sat down at Morehead's desk and, finding paper, pen, and ink, set himself to writing a detailed account of Brayton's involvement in the death of Morton Schaeffer and paying for the murder of Joe Potatoes. It was, as far as Sam knew, the whole truth, and it was written in the form of a confession, using the personal "I" as if Brayton had either written it or dictated it. There was a finishing statement that it was the whole truth and nothing but the truth. A place was left for Brayton's signature and that of a witness. He would never sign this confession, of course, Sam knew, but he wanted it ready. Beyond that, this confession would serve as a summation of events for Wilbarth to read.

Fisher was back a little before train time, and sat in silence while Sam finished. Rising, Sam put on his jacket, put the confession in his pocket, told Fisher to bar anyone from seeing Brayton until he returned, and then left the office.

He crossed the river toward the depot, and was climbing the platform steps as the train whistled for the bridge crossing; a minute later it ground to a sighing halt alongside the platform.

Marshal Wilbarth was the first passenger off the train, and Sam gloomily interpreted this fact as the measure of Wilbarth's anxiousness to take over the situation here. For all the big marshal's recent traveling, his face still had the pallor of that of a man bound indoors against his will. His townsman's suit and overcoat were rumpled, and unless a man was careful to note the calm in his pale eyes, he appeared to be only another uncared-for and probably lazy old man.

They shook hands and Sam asked, "Did Joe talk, Marshal?"

"Not a word. We had to give up on him, Sam."

Sam took his valise and steered him to the Primrose House hack. Only after he registered did Sam say, "I know it's early, Marshal, but how about a drink?"

Wilbarth grimaced. "I've had enough of that stuff in the last ten days to float a frigate, but the answer is yes."

In the saloon, which held only a handful of customers, Sam chose the table nearest the front window. Sam received a bottle and two glasses and some cigars from Alec, and when he turned back to the table, he saw that Wilbarth was rubbing his closed eyelids with thumb and index finger in a gesture of unutterable weariness. His hat was on the table and his white hair seemed overlong, as if he had not had time for a visit to a barber recently.

Sam sat down, took the confession from his jacket pocket, and handed it to Wilbarth. "That's a confession I wrote out for Brayton to sign. He won't sign it, of course, but it will bring you up to date on Brayton's connivings here."

Wilbarth set the paper aside for the present and said, "First tell me how you got that piece in the *Capital Times* about arresting Joe Potatoes."

It took Sam until dinnertime to bring Wilbarth up to date. He told of Tenney's visit to Junction City to warn him of an almost certain ambush. His planting of false information with Red Macandy had been intended to accomplish just what it had — flush Carnes out. The rest of it was distasteful, but Sam went through it doggedly. Carnes, probably hurt, had escaped, and without him and with Herrington dead, the case against Brayton was weak, he said. If Joe remained silent, it was no case at all. To all this, Wilbarth listened with neither censure nor approval in his face.

At dinnertime, Sam introduced Wilbarth to Louise Selby and her father, and only moments later to Tenney. Standing by the table and shaking Tenney's hand, Wilbarth said, "So you're the little lady we're indebted to?"

Tenney blushed, but before she could say anything, Wilbarth continued, "I'd like to meet your mother too, Miss Payne, but this wouldn't be the time, would it?"

"No, I don't think so," Tenney agreed.

"Later, then," Wilbarth said.

They had the usual good meal, and afterwards they went back to the courthouse for an afternoon session with Brayton. Sam took the precaution of buying a quart of whiskey from Alec. As he put it in his jacket's side pocket under the puzzled gaze of Wilbarth, he said, "Without this, I don't think Con Brayton can even talk."

Twenty-Three

Sometime in the middle of that gray afternoon, it came abruptly to Seeley Carnes, lying in his stinking cot, that he had a way to get at Sam Kennery. It had been there all the time, but he'd been too thick-headed to see it. At peace now, he turned over and went to sleep immediately.

The night shift left for work, and the miners from the day shift began to flee the tent for the saloons. Again Carnes tried to find an honest face to buy him food and liquor. He had made a wrong guess; this time the miner to whom he gave the money showed up an hour afterwards, drunk and with no food. He tried with another of the tent inmates. This time he was brought his late sandwich and another pint of whiskey. Afterwards, he let the evening drift into deep night before he stirred.

After putting on his boots, he rose, took his gun and cartridge belt from his mackinaw, and strapped it on. Leaving his lunch bucket under the cot, he left the tent. A big kerosene flare burned beyond the entrance of the tent, a beacon for the reveling miners. He walked slowly now, trying out his leg. On this side of the river he knew he would not be recognized, and he made his slow way up River Street to the bridge, ignoring the drunken miners who crowded him off the boardwalk onto the street. He skirted one street fight and then paused on the bridge to rest. So far, so good.

Minutes later, Carnes moved on up toward the deserted Grant Street. There were a few store night lights burning, but at this hour, the town on this side of the river was asleep. The only noise came from the river and from the whiskey festivities on the other side of it.

When Carnes, his pace slow but steady, came up to the Primrose House veranda, he paused and saw that it was deserted. There was a night light by the bell on the lobby desk. The doors would be open to accommodate late travelers, he knew. As he passed the saloon, he saw that it was dark and only then did he realize that it was really late. At the corner of the Primrose House he turned right and headed down the alley, passing the loading bay, and halted at the corner of the building beyond it. Yes, the rain barrel was there, a symbol of the humiliation he was about to revenge.

Now, from his left-hand mackinaw pocket, he took out a couple of matches. Most of the day he had debated what he was going to do next. From his quick search of the women's rooms before Kennery had charged in to start the fight that night, he knew that the door to the right in the bedroom was the entrance to the kitchen. He knew this because he had opened it, just as he had opened the door to the closet in the opposite wall. That night the door to the kitchen had been locked with a key left in the lock, and he supposed it would be locked tonight. Once he was inside, he must beat them to that door.

Now he moved forward, halting at the alley door, and knocked softly. He was remembering Sam Kennery's words, which he had overheard the night of the fight, so that when the girl's sleepy voice asked who was there, Carnes said, "It's me, Sam. Open up, Tenney." He counted on the door's thickness to blur his voice, just as it blurred hers. He heard the key in the lock turn now, and waited until the door started to swing open. He pushed into it with his shoulder then, and it bumped the girl, who stepped back, startled. With a single sweep of his arm, he moved in, grasped her around the waist, and kicked the door shut behind him, just as she cried out.

Lifting her, he hobbled as fast as he could into the bedroom. He was already through the bedroom door when Mrs. Payne called, "Tenney! Tenney! What is it?"

Carnes put the kicking, struggling girl down, and with his left hand he struck the two matches against the wall. In their sudden flare he saw Tenney standing there in her nightgown, pure terror in her face. Mrs. Payne had thrown the covers off and was standing between the two beds, a look of fear and anger in her face.

"Light that lamp and be quick about it," Carnes said. He watched Mrs. Payne turn, take a match from the dish beside the lamp on the table between the two beds, strike it, lift the chimney, and light the lamp. When it was lighted, Carnes dropped his matches and lifted his gun from its holster.

"What do you want with us, Mr. Carnes?" Tenney said.

Seeley didn't answer immediately. He looked around the room, and then his glance fell to the bed, where Tenney's gray wrapper lay at its foot. "Put that on," he said.

"What are you going to do?" Tenney demanded.

"It's not me that'll do anything, it's you. Put it on."

Tenney looked at her mother, who said, "Do it, Tenney."

Tenney slipped into the wrapper and tied its belt. Now Carnes moved to the kitchen door, felt for its key, and lifted it out. "Now you, lady," he said to Mrs. Payne. "Climb over that bed, get in the closet, and close the door."

"Not until I know what you're going to do," Mrs. Payne said flatly.

"I'm taking Tenney on a trip."

"Kidnap her, you mean?"

"For ten minutes maybe," Carnes said quietly. "She'll be back and let you out."

"I won't go with you!" Tenney said.

Carnes looked at her and asked unsmilingly, "Is Morehead dead?"

"Dying," Tenney said.

"I shot him," Carnes said. "I killed Mort Schaeffer. If they catch me, I'll hang. I won't hang any higher if I kill you. You hear that, don't you?"

"What is it you want?" Tenney asked tremblingly.

Carnes ignored her, looking at her mother. He gestured with his gun. "In the closet, lady."

Helpless and furious, Mrs. Payne climbed over Tenney's bed, opened the closet door, and stepped into it, closing it behind her.

Now Carnes signaled again with his revolver, saying to Tenney, "Get over there."

Tenney backed over to the kitchen door and watched helplessly as Carnes, gun in hand, manhandled the heavy dresser up against the closet door. Then he came back to Tenney.

"Go into the dining room, through it, and upstairs," Carnes said. "Don't make any noise. Now move. I'll be behind you."

"What do I do up there?" Tenney asked.

"Go to Kennery's room. Knock on his door and call him. I know his room. It's the front corner one. Don't try and pick an empty room and hammer on the door till you wake the whole hotel. I'll be a foot behind you all the time."

"Kennery's gone," Tenney said.

For answer, Carnes gave her a stinging, backhanded clout across the cheek and mouth. "You're lying. I saw him." He raised his hand again. "Now do you still say he's gone?" Tenney shook her head, her hand pressed against her cheek. "Then get going."

Tenney led the way out of the kitchen, through the dark dining room only faintly lit by the lobby lamp, and through the glass doors, where she turned. Without halting, she started to climb the stairs. She could hear Carnes' labored breathing as they climbed. He was hurt, she knew, but she didn't know where.

She had accepted Carnes' blow in the kitchen after failing to make him believe Kennery had left. She had admitted lying, and she knew that now she was nearing her last chance to save Sam. Sam was not in the room Carnes had named, and when Carnes discovered it, what would she do? What could she do?

On the second-floor landing, she turned left and walked quietly down the corridor. Carnes followed. The wall lamp at that end of the corridor was the nearest one to Sam's room, and lit the corridor faintly but clearly. At the door of Sam's room she stopped so abruptly that Carnes bumped into her, his pistol jabbing her in the back.

"What do I say?" she whispered.

Carnes whispered back, "Say 'Sam, let me in. Something's happened!'"

"Do I knock?"

"I do," Carnes said.

Reaching around her, he knocked firmly on the door. Then he looked at Tenney and nodded. Tenny called out as loudly as she dared, "Sam, Sam, let me in! Something's happened!"

They waited, but no sound came from the room. Carnes leaned across her to knock again on the door.

Tenney looked over his shoulder at the door of Brayton's room, the one that Sam was occupying. It was closed.

Now Carnes drew back and nodded to her again. This time, risking everything, Tenney called loudly, "Sam! Sam! Let me in! Something's happened!"

Carnes gave her a ferocious scowl, and she felt the gun press into her back.

And then Kennery's voice came from behind her, saying sharply, "Drop, Tenney!"

As Carnes wheeled at the sound of Kennery's voice, Tenney sank to the floor. A shot, followed immediately by another shot, blasted out in deafening twin explosions, and Tenney felt Carnes' boots drive against her huddled body, heard his bulk slam against the wall above her, and then, with a gagging sigh, slide sideways down the wall and hit the floor with a heavy, muffled thud.

Fearfully, Tenney looked up and saw that Sam, stripped to the waist, was unmarked by blood; he started to stride toward her, and a torrent of relief swept over her. If he had been hit, he couldn't come to her. She struggled to her feet and was engulfed in Sam's arms. She held him tightly to her, fighting back the hysteria that made her want to scream with relief.

"Tenney, Tenney," Sam murmured "Thank God, thank God he didn't kill you."

Now the doors down the corridor began to open. Wilbarth, his pants pulled on over his nightshirt, came out of Herrington's old room, gun in hand. He saw Kennery holding Tenney, and then his glance shuttled to the figure on the floor.

"That's Carnes, Marshal. He came to the wrong room with Tenney as a shield, and tried to make her toll me to the door."

Now other men came from far rooms, all in various stages of undress. Sam said to Tenney, "Steady now. We've got to make sure he's dead." He left her and joined Wilbarth, who had rolled Carnes on his back. Sam's shot had caught him high in the chest, smashing into his heart. Carnes' shot, which had ripped into the floor at Sam's feet, must have been pure reflex, for Carnes must have died instantly. Wilbarth rose and told the half-dozen men who were gathered around, "This is a hunted killer you're looking at. He's dead, but take a look at him if you want. Then please go back to your rooms."

Sam rose now, went back to Tenney, led her into his dark room, lighted the lamp, and led her to a chair, where he told her to sit down. He picked up his shirt now, and while he was putting it on, he said, "Tell me about it, Tenney." As he dressed, Tenney told him almost incoherently of Carnes' break-in, the locking up of her mother, and his forcing her to lead him to the room Carnes remembered as Kennery's room. She had hoped beyond hope that her call to him would be loud enough to wake him, and it had.

Sam wondered if either of them would ever know how close to death they had been. If a precautionary whim had not made him decide this morning to change his room, or if Tenney had been frightened enough to take Carnes to Brayton's room, he, instead of Carnes, would be lying dead out in the hall.

Sam swept the blanket from his bed, then held out a hand to Tenney and eased her to her feet. "Let's go to your mother," he said.

Out in the ball, he threw the blanket over Carnes and was turning away when Tenney said, "The key's in his pocket, Sam."

Sam knelt beside the body, pulled out Carnes' doeskin pouch of stinking tobacco, felt below it, and found the key. He heard footsteps on the stairs then and rose, looking down the hall. Mr. Selby and Louise stepped from the stairs into the corridor, and at the same moment, Wilbarth, dressed in his townsman's suit, came out of his room. Taking Tenney by the elbow, Sam said to Wilbarth, "Tell the Selbys what happened, Marshal, then come down into the kitchen."

As they approached the halted Selbys, Sam said, "The marshal will tell you about it, Mr. Selby. We've got to hurry."

Tenney walked ahead of him, and he was on the stairs before he realized he still held Carnes' doeskin tobacco pouch. He would have thrown it away if there had been anyplace to throw it, but there wasn't, so he rammed it in his jacket pocket.

Tenney hurried through the kitchen doors, pausing long enough to turn up the lamp so Sam had light enough to put in the key, and then they both approached the door to the Payne women's rooms. After unlocking it, Sam moved swiftly across the bedroom to the closet, wrestled the dresser away from it, and opened the door. Mrs. Payne rushed past him into Tenney's arms. She had been crying, Sam saw. He walked past them into the kitchen, swinging the door partially shut behind him.

Moving slowly into the kitchen, Sam thought, *This cleans it all up — except for Brayton.* Without Carnes to bargain with if he gave evidence against Brayton, the agent would very likely go free. Neither the purchase of one murder nor the attempted purchase of another, nor criminal fraud could be proven against him. All the witnesses except the silent Joe Potatoes were dead.

Then, abruptly, Sam stopped his pacing. He remembered that Brayton, in their first conversation in the jail, had momentarily been tempted to sign a confession. Only the fact that Brayton was sure Carnes couldn't be caught to testify against him had led him to brazen it out.

At that moment, Louise Selby, followed by Wilbarth and Mr. Selby, came into the kitchen. Sam caught Wilbarth's attention and beckoned to him as the Selbys went into the bedroom.

"That cleans us up, Sam," the Marshal said wearily. "There are questions you'll have to answer, but this cleans us up."

"Not quite," Sam reminded him. "There's Brayton."

"If he misses conviction, he'll be ruined anyway."

"Maybe he won't miss it," Sam said. "Do you have that confession with you?"

Wilbarth slapped his side pockets and then his upper coat pockets. Hearing the crackle of paper, he reached into an inside coat pocket and brought out the confession Sam had drafted that morning.

"Would we be proper witnesses to this confession, Marshal?"

"Yes. But as a matter of course, his lawyers will claim he was forced to sign it."

"Would a third witness help?" Sam pursued.

"I'd judge so. But you won't get him to sign it anyway, Sam. You've talked with him and I've talked with him, until we're both hoarse. What good's it done?"

"Things are different now, maybe," Sam said quietly. "Wait here a minute." Sam moved over to the door of the Payne women's bedroom, where Mrs. Payne was seated on the bed, telling the Selbys of Carnes' break-in.

Tenney was listening, but when Sam moved into the doorway she looked at him and smiled. Beckoning her to him, Sam stepped back into the kitchen when she joined him, he said, "Tenney, can you get dressed now? We're paying Brayton a visit. We need you again."

"Of course. It's almost daylight anyway."

Sam and Wilbarth waited in the kitchen until Tenney, having dressed in the living room, came to join them, her coat over her arm. Sam led the way out through the dining room lobby to the street, and their walk to the courthouse was a silent one.

In the courthouse corridor, while Tenney and Wilbarth waited, Sam roused Matt Fisher to let him in. When the door was opened for him, Sam said, "Go back to bed, Matt. I'm only after pen and ink and the cell key."

He crossed to the desk and took pen and ink from it, and after taking the cell key from the nail behind the door, he joined Wilbarth and Tenney in the hall. Putting a hand on the doorknob of the cell block stairs, Sam hesitated. "Remember, let me do the talking — all the talking. Either of you might spoil it with one word."

They both nodded now, and Sam swung open the door and led the way down the steps into the cell block. Brayton, under his blankets, was awakened by the noise of their descent and was sitting up looking at them when Sam turned up the wick of the lamp.

"You again," Brayton said sourly.

Sam moved over to unlock the cell door, the keys in one hand, the confession, pen, and ink in the other.

He stepped inside, leaving the door open. "Yes, me again, Con," Sam said. "Not everybody gets a last chance like you're getting."

"Last chance for what?"

"To sign this confession."

"I told you I wouldn't sign it!" Brayton said irritably. "I told you a thousand times!"

"Well, you've got one more chance, Con." He paused to isolate what he was about to say. "We've got Carnes. They're bringing him in."

"I don't believe it!" Brayton said.

Sam reached in his pocket and brought out Carnes pouch of stinking tobacco. "We found that when we searched him. Recognize it?"

Brayton picked up the pouch, smelled it, made a face, and tossed it on his blanket. He said nothing.

"Remember the afternoon I locked you up? We had a talk, Con. I told you if we caught Carnes, we'd offer him a trade. We'd ask for a life sentence instead of hanging, if he'd give evidence against you. Well, we've got him."

"Is he talking?"

"No."

"He never will," Brayton said.

"Want to bet an extra five years in prison he won't, Con?"

The agent was silent for a long moment, studying the hump his feet made in the blankets "Got a drink?" he asked.

"Not this time, Con. Nobody can claim we got you drunk enough to sign it. This has got to be your dead sober choice."

"I haven't even got a lawyer!" Brayton protested.

"By the time you get one, they'll have brought Carnes in."

"Too late, you mean."

"I would judge, but I leave it up to you."

"I never trusted that damn Texan!" Con said viciously. "He'll make this all my idea from start to finish. It wasn't."

"Last chance, Con," Sam said almost idly. "We've got to take care of Carnes. You read the confession this afternoon. Sign it or don't sign it. Don't sign and face your twelve fools; sign and face your one educated fool, the judge." When Brayton was silent, Sam said, "Good night, Con."

He turned and headed for the cell door.

"Come back here!" Brayton snarled. "Let me read the damn thing again!" Sam handed him the confession, then went out into the hall, took down the lamp from its bracket, and came into the cell with it. He did not look at Wilbarth or Tenney, who were watching all of this in mute wonder.

While Brayton read the document by the light of the lamp held by Sam, the room was so quiet they could hear the distant mill sounds. When he was finished reading it, Brayton gave a shuddering sigh. Then he said in a weary voice, "All right, I'll sign it."

Sam extended the pen and uncorked the bottle of ink. He lifted the pile of the *Capital Times* beside Con's cot, folded them until they made a stiff enough support to write on, and handed them to Brayton.

"Come in, Tenney, Marshal," Sam called. The small girl and the big man filed into the cell and watched as Brayton signed the confession. Sam then dated the confession and noted the approximate hour of signing; then, in turn, he signed, Tenney signed, and Wilbarth signed as witnesses. Sam said to Wilbarth, "You keep that, Marshal." He turned and picked up the lamp from the floor. "I think you'll sleep better now, Con."

The three of them filed out of the cell block, and while Wilbarth returned the lamp to its bracket and turned down the wick, Sam locked the cell.

"Good night Con."

The agent grunted.

Tenney started up the steps, and Sam waited for Wilbarth to precede him. Then Brayton called from the cell, "Sam, wait! Will they put Carnes in my cell when they bring him in?"

Tenney and Wilbarth halted, looking down at Sam.

Sam turned and looked at Brayton. "No, Con. They'll bury him. He's dead, you see."

The employees of G.K. HALL hope you have enjoyed this Large Print book. All our Large Print titles are designed for easy reading, and all our books are made to last. Other G.K. Hall Large Print books are available at your library, through selected bookstores, or directly from us. For more information about current and upcoming titles, please call or mail your name and address to:

G.K. HALL
PO Box 159
Thorndike, Maine 04986
800/223-6121
207/948-2962